THE UNCANNY VALLEY CLUB

The Uncanny Valley Club

WHERE ALL YOUR DREAMS COME TRUE

Julie
Proudfoot

Powerful Owl Press

Contents

To Wayne

Trigger Warning
This work of fiction contains acts of violence and sexual
violence.

1

Henry

A loud, hollow thump comes to Henry's attention from across the circuit, and when he looks, he sees a pedestrian fall to the bitumen road—with arms spread out and legs stiffened in fright, Jesus-style —stalling the honking traffic. A woman comes forward and bends a knee to the road by the pedestrian's side. She looks up, this woman, and shouts threats at the receding self-drive while holding her phone high to record its cold-hearted retreat.

A crowd gathers, drawn to an opportunity to air grievances, and they, too, reach up with their phones, as though in a synchronised Nazi salute, to film the self-drive as it tootles down the road, off and away, without a care.

The entire shenanigans seeming to be a result of the self-drive having selected the path of least damage: up the curb, onto the foot-path, and neatly into a lone and oblivious pedestrian—thump.

She speaks to the body still laying on the road—this woman who Henry will come to know, and come to know well— and the laid-out body raises an arm and gestures, so this time, Henry is relieved to see, there's no fatality.

Henry turns his back on the commotion, and he grips Vince's wheelchair and thrusts him forward. Vince glides with his arms raised playfully in the air, then directs himself through the sliding doors that close behind him, squeezing cooled air back toward Henry on the footpath.

Henry holds his face up to the sun. Above him, the upper and lower traffic streams hum in orderly lanes and cut interrupted shadows across his eyes. Wildflowers throw lush scents down from the rooftop gardens, and Henry opens his car door, tugging it hard against the rusted hinges of his petrol-driven Mini. He climbs in, starts the car with a tug of the choke, and heads off around the circuit, past the dispersing crowd and the arriving ambulance to the nearby bus terminal to pick up the latest intern to work at Quinn Robotics Corp (QRC).

2

Henry

Henry presses his phone to his ear. There are nine missed calls from Benny—that's frantic behaviour, even for Benny. The first message is tentative and awkward: 'Hey Henry, I think I have a plan for you. It might help with your Little Problem. It could be a total reset—' And then he hung up before he'd finished speaking, which was a good decision because he didn't make a lot of sense.

This is new; Benny may be awkward, but he's never tentative. At his meekest, Benny is a bulldozer. The second message from Benny has a revised tone, like a real estate agent about to close a deal: 'Henry! Call me! I have a new direction for you! I've found you a fix! Call me!'

Benny and his cures are a thing to avoid. He creates projects out of nowhere, most likely to give the impression—generally intended for Quinn—that he's busy. And in that vein, he's built Henry's problem up to be much bigger than it is. To return Benny's call will be to listen to yet another story about Benny's cures. It's company policy that Henry speaks with Benny; that is, Benny the therapist, not Benny in his other role: Benny the sex-bot salesman.

Benny's avatar lights up on Henry's phone, indicating seven more calls to listen to. Benny's avatar is one he uses for all his socials and best described as 'interesting'. Henry maintains a distance from Benny's private socials—they're kind of icky. The only time Henry accepted an invitation to view Benny's video stream, he copped a glimpse of who Benny is when he's at home. And Benny was not who Henry thought he was.

Henry has come to the conclusion that Benny must think of him as a friend—because nobody should witness that weird display of hobbies. Henry deletes the seven remaining calls.

'Call Benny,' he says into his phone.

The call goes to voicemail. Benny's recorded voice is monotone with an occasional high-pitched crack that sneaks in now and then, like he's a twelve-year-old boy.

'It's Henry,' he says, 'Sorry I missed your calls. I got caught up with the usual. I'll call again next Monday.' He slides the hang-up before Benny can catch him, then puts his phone deep into his pocket to avoid hearing any further calls.

In the next room, the tiny doors of the orange cuckoo clock pop open with the squeak of a hinge. He flinches, as though Benny himself has launched through the wall. The cuckoo blurts seven squawks—hideous, but lovable. It was a gift from Quinn. That's what Quinn does—he gives gifts when he wants your attention.

Henry is out of bed and into the lounge in time to watch the colourful bird wobble on the uneven tracks as it creeps back into its little house. The cuckoo's door slaps shut like a sharp clap, and the tiny bird will stay quiet now until its next shift begins. Its predictability, as always, is a comfort to Henry.

≈

Henry takes a pack of antibacterial wipes from his pocket and passes one over the number pad in the lift. He pushes the ground-floor button and presses his back to the wall. The floors slide past—220, 219, 218—and he holds his phone up to check the signal, and then touches Esther's avatar.

'What?' she asks, by way of an answer. Esther isn't a word-waster.

'Esther, what time does the intern come in?'

'I'll throw you the folder now,' she says.

'Email it to me, will you?'

'Henry, tell me you have plans to get your dots. It's embarrassing that you haven't got them yet.'

Henry has resisted getting his dots. Humans and bots sharing the same connected tech doesn't make sense to him. It's not even clear what the consequences of this might be. The convenience and fun of it seems to blot out any idea that it might not be a good thing for humanity, and nobody seems to care.

'Yeah, I know; one day I'll get them,' he lies.

'I'll tell you something, Henry: there are so many enhancements you could be using to get your life on the free and easy. I wouldn't be without any of it, and I never dreamed I'd be feeling so amazing at my age.'

Henry has known Esther way more than ten years, and if he's recalling correctly, she's never mentioned her actual age, which is probably irrelevant as he's certain she's not all real. She's a big fan of Scottie Fuennel's cyborg enhancements, and she's had parts switched out so many times—which possibly range in age from teenager to something approaching a century—that she's probably not even certain of her own age either.

'Yesterday, I was, like, dropping dead,' Esther explains. 'You think about your age when you tick one over, right? And to be honest, I've been feeling pretty shitty. So, I go to the doctor. And guess what? I've been worried for no reason.'

'Worried?'

'Yes, for no reason at all. I'm not even sure I should share this with you, Henry. Have you heard of Blood Soldiers? A little bit of me, a little bit of technology.'

'Blood Soldiers? Never heard of it.'

'It's a treatment, with soldiers suspended in it.'

'Sounds like you *should* be worried.'

'It's like penicillin, only—'

'Only tiny little men with helmets?' Henry queries.

'Of course not, but tiny, yes, and then off they go the little fuckers, to seek out their targeted cells.'

'Is this new? Who did you get it from?'

Esther doesn't reply.

'Was it Scottie? Don't let Quinn find out.'

'I don't care what Quinn thinks; Quinn's all talk. I think I'm the only person Quinn doesn't scare.'

'So, you have tiny men inside you, dismantling your cells for the rest of your life?'

'Gross, I know. But no, they deactivate in fifty days and expel the usual way. Job done.' Esther laughs.

'You poop the soldiers?'

They're both silent for a beat, taking that information in. Henry watches the lift numbers tick by—140, 139, 138.

'I think this conversation is over, Henry.'

'It's your birthday?' he asks, thankful for a shift in subject.

'Yes, it's my fucking birthday. How do you not know this? You're supposed to be my friend.'

'Happy birthday to you, Esther. I mean it.' He makes a mental note to organise a gift for her, but what to get for somebody as dynamic as Esther? He's never sure.

'Are we going to be partners at this karaoke thing next week?' she asks.

'I'm not going this time. There's never any fun in it.'

'You *are* going. You have to go. I'm not singing on my own.'

'I think we're supposed to bond at these things, but do we bond? Really? I think we all just hate each other a little bit more.'

Henry will go to karaoke night. He always does, but saying he won't go feels so good. It's the most defiant he can be in the face of Quinn's control. He lets the idea percolate in his thoughts and imagines not turning up to sing. He imagines Quinn's blotchy face, red with annoyance. And then he imagines having to find a new job because Quinn won't stand for that. This negative way of thinking about his job has become a habit—a comforting habit, but a bad habit. He needs to stop it.

'You know partners are welcome, right?' Henry says. 'Why not take Billy, Esther?'

At a previous work event, Billy sat there like an angry little gnome, his face a twisted fight of forced smiles. Billy is a little bit above karaoke. Billy doesn't deserve Esther.

'You don't take anybody with you,' Esther says.

'I don't have anyone.'

'You don't have anyone for longer than a minute, you mean.'

Henry holds back on making comments about Esther's partner. He has a sense, which may be guilt, that it's his responsibility as her friend to let her know what a parasite Billy is, but the amount of pain that knowledge would cause her has so far superseded his responsibility to tell her. One day, he hopes the opportunity to imply Billy's cheating will conveniently appear in the conversation.

Esther talks on about Henry's difficulty with relationships, his selfishness, his awkward manner and how it all relates back to his Little Problem. When she says the words 'Little Problem', he zones out. This attachment everybody around him has to his relationship issues as a conversation piece has got out of hand.

Behind him, between the walls, the spiralling steel ropes smash against the lift shaft. The floor numbers flash past—89, 88, 87. He imagines the lift flying free though the clouds, like the old movie *Charlie and the Chocolate Factory*.

Through the phone, Esther mumbles something about the intern. 'Here,' she adds, 'your intern arrives in the station at 7:30 this morning.'

'Give them a call, will you? Tell them I'll be late.'

'I'll get them to wait at the bus terminal.'

'Thank you, Esther. You've always got my back'

'I've got everyone's back. It's my job, remember? To rub out transgressions, even your little mishaps. Are you in the lift, Henry?'

Henry hangs up on her. She knows he has a daily fight with this lift. If he'd let her go on, she'd rehash her old commentary: if he owned an elevation car, like anyone else in his position, he wouldn't need to use the broken-down lift. Then, she'll say he should give up his upper-tier apartment if he's not going to get an elevation car.

What she actually means when she says this is that he should give up his upper-tier apartment *to her*. He imagines selling it to Esther and moving out of the city, maybe to somewhere quiet. Esther longs for an upper-tier apartment. She already owns an elevation car—in constant hope of obtaining the apartment.

Henry peers at the yellowing sunlight as it wobbles across the lift glass. He presses a palm to the wall to brace for the idiosyncrasies of the lift as it makes its closing descent—19, 18, 17, 16. Henry's thoughts go to his home town, to dappled sunlight and the peppery scent of rubbed wet grass on the football oval, to slow traffic outside the indie supermarket where he worked on Saturdays as a teenager, and the shoe squeaks of the netball game that he paused to watch on his slow walk home, where the goalie on the other end of his future Little Problem would reach to block a shot.

The lift slides on—7, 6, 5—vibrations from the wall move through his hand into his chest. He thinks of muddy streets, and tyres that hang from ropes. He thinks of evening television and foggy dribbles on windows, and he thinks of his father. He wonders what his father would look like these days. It's been a long time.

The lift slows to the familiar level two. Henry hits the button with the back of his hand. With Esther having sorted out the intern for him, he's gained extra time to make a visit.

The lift comes to a stop with a sway. The glass vibrates, the floor careens, and the lift leans and settles. The tiny buttons in the wall move inside their perfectly round holes. Henry breathes out as the door slides open. Stepping forward, he arrives at Vince's front door.

3

Benny & Scottie

Benny makes his way down the hallway of Fuennel Industries, walking close to the wall, and he comes to stand in the doorway of Scottie's office, where he finds her seated, and focussed on her screen. He has his own way of getting in this building, unnoticed, and Scottie turns a blind eye to this; she turns a blind eye to much of what he does, and he's happy to take advantage of her leniency, he likes to think of it as affection.

He shifts his weight quietly from foot to foot; meek shuffling sounds rise from the floor. 'Scottie,' he says, 'I'd like to tell you all about my new business.'

She glances at him. 'I'll be with you in a minute, Benny,' she says, but stays seated at her desk and ignores him. Benny doesn't understand how she does this; people don't ignore him—he goes out of his way to make sure of it.

'I've named it The Uncanny Valley Club.' He talks to her back as though it's a wall he can penetrate with a catchy phrase. He imagines a dance to go with it: a slap of the foot and jazz hands. The Uncanny Valley Club! The name itself will pique her interest, for sure.

'You could make an appointment like a normal person, Benny,' she says.

She's right, of course, but if the situation were reversed, he wouldn't keep her waiting like this. In his bot-sales business, he's available day or night, weekend or not, like it or not. Admittedly, his clients are fickle and emotionally driven, and not attending to his clients instantly means losing their business, instantly.

He reads Scottie's screen over her shoulder. She's working on a journal article. The title is 'Blood Soldiers'. She brings her hands to her neck in thought and attacks her tie with long fingers. She twists it and pats it down, twists it up again, and then leans into her screen.

'My new club—it'll blow your mind,' Benny declares, loudly this time.

Scottie says nothing; absolutely nothing. She knows he can't stand it, the waiting. There's not much Scottie doesn't know. She's curious that way. She's across everything, about everybody that happens in this city; this is what he knows about her, and he'll use this information to leverage a commitment from her today. He's come to hold the view that, to get her to invest in his business, his best plan is to suggest the idea of a partnership: equal control. She'll be sweetened by the possibility of control. With his hands in his pockets, Benny slides his foot across the floor and sits in the only other chair in the room.

He has an urge to scream his excitement for his new project into her face, instead, he touches behind his ear and tunes in to his music to settle his thoughts. When Scottie does decide to give him some of her time, he doesn't hear her immediately. He becomes aware that she's trying to get his attention, waving her hand in his face. He flicks his tunes off.

'This idea of yours, Benny, explain it to me.'

He comes alive and scoots his chair over to her side. 'Scottie, listen, I'm looking for an investor, but more than that, I'm looking for a silent partner. I'm ready to go on it. All I really need is the money to kick it off, and not to get too vulgar on you, Scottie, but you'd be the money part of this deal.' He points at her with a finger-and-thumb gun. 'And that's all you need to think about.' He waits, watches her blank eyes, then lowers his finger-and-thumb gun slowly to his lap.

'That's all you've got to say, Benny? You've waited here patiently like a silly goose, and that's it? I'm not even sure what it is you're trying to tell me.'

'I know you like to keep things simple, Scott, so it boils down to this: I'm expanding my business, and I'd love you to come on board.' He smiles at his generous invitation. 'Just you,' he adds, to point her away from the fact that it's not only her that he's approached to join his business. 'With me,' he concludes, because who wouldn't want the privilege of joining him in business.

Scottie smiles evenly and nods. 'Benny, a minute ago, you said it'd blow my mind. What will? What'll blow my mind? We're old friends, so I'm going to help you out here. Let me assume that this club has nothing at all to do with those sex dolls you palm off for Quinn. You wouldn't bring that to me, would you? And since I'm helping you, I want you to help me. Tell me why I'll like your idea. I'm helping you, see? See me helping you, Benny?' Scottie leans back in her seat and reaches behind her for a cup on her desk. Taking a sip, she beckons with her hand, inviting his response, as though they're engaged in a friendly debate.

'Scott, my girls are more than sex dolls. I'm insulted you'd call them that, and they'd be insulted, too. In my therapy work we call them "social robots" .' Benny holds back an urge to call out her misplaced principles. Her feminist ideals are the thing that'll colour her decision here today, but he can't help himself, he needs her to know that he understands her. 'And there's no need for you to get your conscience dirty, Scottie. You don't need to involve yourself in the cogs of the process. I'm only here about the solid investment.'

It's not news to him that sex bots aren't Scottie's thing, but there's value in this for her: control and money, and if Scottie loves anything, it's control and money. He has a hunch she won't let slide an opportunity to control a robot business, especially if it's possible that her only competitor, Quinn, will have a grab at it too. 'And a partnership, of course, Scottie. That's it: money and partnership.' Benny rolls his chair backward to give them both thinking space.

'So, it does involve Quinn's sex dolls,' she says.

'Don't be like that, Scott; these bots are the future of therapy. They're chicken soup for the troubled soul, a balm to desire, a witness to ailment. They're needed; they're essential. You don't need to be afraid of them—they're honest and reliable.'

She smiles and takes another sip. 'I'm not afraid of your bots, Benny, but I *am* afraid that your "chicken soup for the troubled soul" is just another way of validating abuse.' She pokes her words at him with her finger. 'Your use of those bots in your various businesses are all opportunities to reshape that intimate human moment—a moment of connection, of love—into something cold-hearted. And there's no chicken soup for the soul in sight.'

'Listen, let's back it up a bit. I'm not here to argue with you. I'm here to make you a sound business offer. To be honest, your rejection of robots shows you to be way out of touch. You're missing out on lucrative opportunities. Relationships with robots are programmed and predictable, and it's irresponsible of you to lead people to believe it's anything less desirable than that. I've read your blog, I follow your little protest group, and I disagree with you. I don't believe for a second that what happens between a person and their bot has any influence on their human relationships—what happens in Vegas stays in Vegas. Humans *socialise* with humans, but humans *operate* robots—and those scenarios have nothing to do with each other.'

'You're so wrong, Benny. What happens in Vegas changes everything at home. How can it not? Every experience changes us, and every experience with a bot changes the way we relate to the people around us.'

Benny sighs and slumps in his chair. He's allowed Scottie to ambush the conversation. 'Let's get back to the money. You front the money,' he says, and he touches his finger to her desk to pin the idea down in her thoughts, 'and you'll never be sorry. This investment will come back to you tenfold. And there'll be control over parts of my business for you as an investor.'

Three days ago, Benny had used this exact line on Quinn. Quinn said he'd invest, but only if Scottie invested first, and then Quinn collapsed into his chair laughing at the impossibility of the idea. It was his way of saying no to Benny without actually having to say no, because, of course, Scottie would never come on board with a sex-doll brothel. Benny had taken it as a challenge and noted the simple facts: if he can get Scottie to invest, then Quinn will too, and, he will hold Quinn to his word.

'And seriously, Scott, look at me sitting here all composed, while inside, I'm screaming with the ex-ci-tation of it all. This is a great opportunity for us. If you don't get on board with this, I won't hesitate to take my idea elsewhere.'

'And who would you take your idea to, Benny? To Quinn?'

Benny shrugs. The truth is that he needs more than cash to get this business off the ground. He needs everything Quinn can offer—his business connections, access to his advanced bots, not to mention his sway with council, which he'll need when it comes to getting his building approved—and at this point, it all hinges on getting Scottie to come on board.

'I know you'll put this idea to Quinn; I mean, who else is there? He's the only sex-bot producer in the state. You'd be stupid not to. But if it's money you want, why don't you float it in the business sector? I'm sure you'll find a fool down there happy to back you.'

'Well, nah, Scottie, it's you that I want on board—your knowledge and your business ethic. You're somebody I can trust.'

Scottie snorts a laugh. She's bound to be privy to his failures and debts, and no doubt enjoys watching him squirm. 'If you plan to use sex dolls for this new business, you'll need to sell me an idea that recognises my values a whole lot more than what you've put on the table.'

Benny smiles in an attempt to appear to care about Scottie's views. 'Yes, my girls will play a part, but the club will employ the bots, not enslave them. It's a service—think hospitality. I'm attending to human needs, Scottie; it's as simple as that. We give the people what they need.'

'People are morons.'

'And who are we to get in the way of what the people want? You can't tell me you're not down for making easy money, Scott.' Benny leans in and connects his gaze with hers. 'Money, money, money,' he says, rubbing his fingertips and thumb together.

'Stop talking, Benny.'

She hasn't booted him out of her office—yet. He takes it as a sign he has a foot in the door. He has a great big toe of a chance. 'And this is what I'll do, Scottie, just for you. I'll pay my girls a proper wage, a decent wage.'

Scottie winces. 'Can you not call them "girls" as though you're rounding up chickens? They're autonomous robots who understand what you're doing to them. At least call them what they are.'

'But I own them, so autonomous, I don't—'

'That's not helping, Benn.'

'I'll open a currency account for them, I'll get them insurance, I'll—'

'What kind of insurance?'

For the first time since he arrived in her doorway, Scottie's interest is piqued.

He takes a breath and tempers his answer: 'I'll get them tech insurance, body insurance. Whatever you say they need, Scott; you name it.'

Scottie grins.

Benny wonders what's amused her.

'You pluck these ideas out of that scrubby little head of yours, Benny, and present them gold plated, just to get me on board, but this is no different to an average brothel, is it? I can't see that there's anything special about your new business.'

'Scott, my business is different from *all* the others like it.' Benny waves his hand gently across the room as if to display all the businesses that are just not quite as good as his is. 'It'll be a standout. We can grow a shit load of money from simple human vice. Listen to me. The Uncanny Valley Club will be the venue where punters can set their desires free, like wild animals tapping into their urges.'

'Urges? I thought this was part of your therapy business?'

'It *is* therapy. It's next-level therapy. This is me hitting my potential. This is what I'm all about. I'm dragging the therapy trade into the future.' Benny stands. His excitement at his plans has him all jittery. 'It's not called The Uncanny Valley Club for no reason. It's all about the 'uncanny' moment, that dip in the robot-likeability graph, when you see a robot so lifelike that it gives you the creeps. That hideous little moment that defines the difference between robot and human—the absence of soul, your disgust, your fear and your fascination. It's fake little face.' Benny points at his own eyes and nose, and screws up his face. 'You know what I mean, Scottie; you've felt it. The sense of deceit; the lack of trust. That's where the lucrative Uncanny Valley moment is.'

'Wait a minute, what happened to chicken soup for the soul?'

'Troubled soul, Scottie; I said, "troubled soul". This is the hinge where our clientele swing loose. What a goddamn release! They use it, they respond, they lash out and they release that pent-up techno-anger buried deep within. That little moment is so full of energy! It's a heady mix of fascination and disgust, lust and hate—all those confusing emotions that live in that void. And we will exploit that little, black void of sexuality.'

'Is this a joke, Benny? What kind of place is this?'

'Scottie, nobody trusts a creepy little bot unless they know they control it, right? And how do we take control? We remove human morals. Let them do to it whatever the hell they want to do to it. Our club will give them permission to swing loose. Can't you see it?'

Scottie's mouth hangs open, speechless.

'Listen, Scott, The Uncanny Valley Club will be known as *the* place to explore who we really are at our core.' He leans in to catch her eye. 'The punters can do whatever they like to their bot—no guilt, pure release and morality-free—an almighty cleansing of the soul. Do you see what this is, Scottie? Consequence out the window, do you understand? It's a life-changing moment.'

Scottie's face contorts with disgust.

'Oh, the release,' he says. 'It's so damn freeing.' He lifts his arms into the air as though releasing doves. Benny sees in her face the wall she's built up against this idea. He needs to make her want it. 'And Scottie, let me tell you this much: this will happen whether you like it or not. This isn't new. They exist in Japan and across Europe, and if you get on board with me, right now, you'll control it in our part of the world. You, Scottie. I know this is what you want—to control this industry.'

Scottie says nothing.

He holds his palms out to her and whispers her name. 'Come on, Scott?'

He needs to get her over the line that she's drawn for herself. 'Imagine it, casino atmosphere, private rooms, music and social bots of every colour and proclivity; sturdy ones. You get what I'm saying don't you? I don't need to tell you what people are capable of given the chance. It's exciting! Gives me a buzz just to think about it. All we need is the money. Your money.'

'Why are you giving me this information, Benny? What you're talking about is abuse. All you've done is give me a heads up to intervene and have you shut down. You're an idiot, anyone tell you that?'

'Come on, Scott, you won't do that.'

Scottie turns back to her screen.

It's now clear to Benny that if she's not with him on this, she'll be against it. Having her on board will be integral to getting the club off the ground. Now that she knows about it, he needs to make her say yes. 'Think of it as research, Scottie. There's your inroad right there. You can document this. Let's create it together; let's trial it. I'm thinking Henry. What do you say we trial it on Henry? I have a theory about Henry and his Little Problem. Did you know he has a problem?'

'Everybody knows about Henry's Little Problem,' she says. 'You've been blabbing about it for a long time. I'm not even sure you should call yourself a therapist. Sure, Henry has a problem, but his problem probably starts with you.'

'And it's about to end with me. Quinn has given me the task of getting Henry well, to get him back on track and useful again.'

'Useful to who? You and Quinn?'

'Useful to the company, and useful to himself. Have you seen him? He's kind of in a rut, but our club, Scottie, will help him. He'll be our bunny. After he's immersed himself in it, he'll get his mojo back. You'll see. There's something about tapping into your base self and setting it free. I've seen it with my own eyes. He'll be invincible again. Remember how he used to be? Quinn will get his main guy back in shape, as requested, and you'll get your research. That'll be world recognition for you. And me? I'll get my business fully financed.' Benny smiles. He loves how neatly he's tied this up.

'I'm guessing Henry doesn't have a clue about this?'

'Henry doesn't need to know; this is the beauty of it. Quinn will instruct Henry to canvass the club to make a judgement on whether it's a venue Quinn should support, which it already is, of course. And I'll make sure Henry immerses himself deep in it. I'll give him the full experience. Henry won't think twice about it.'

Scottie flicks through her screens. She's browsing sex-bot venues in Sweden. 'I'd like the details, Benny. It's a nightclub, is it? Sounds squalid, that's what it sounds like. You're not selling it to me at all. Tell me the truth—did you take this Uncanny Valley Club proposal to Quinn first? Did he reject it?'

Benny sways his head slowly in the negative. He quite enjoys lying to her. It's life's thrill—lying, using, getting ahead despite the consensus among them all that he's not savvy enough to be a part of their tribe.

Scottie flips her screen up and raps the desk with her knuckles, twice, to draw his attention. 'Let me explain to you how this'll work, Benny. I'll invest in your club if you do this one thing for me: give me the information about Henry's involvement, every stinking detail about who he speaks to, what he does in this dirty club of yours, how he does it, when he does it and who he does it to.' Scottie gets out of her seat and takes a walk around her office, then comes to stand behind Benny.

'Information on Henry?' Benny queries, without turning to look at her. 'This is your deal, Scott?'

'That's my deal. That's if you actually get this club off the ground. I'm not confident you have it in you, Benn, but if you do, I want footage. I want to own the footage of Henry's visit to this club of yours. You have cameras? I'll invest, but the first thing you'll do for me is make sure your bots have recording devices, and the second thing you'll do for me is make sure those devices record Henry.'

'Scottie, this isn't a fair deal. It's not fair to me, and it's not fair to Henry. You know what'll be on this footage, don't you?'

'If you want the money, you'll do it. Give me a taster. Prove to me that you will. Tell me this: what does Quinn have Henry working on now?' Scottie moves back to her chair, and scrolls her screen with a casual finger, sliding it slowly.

'Now? Scottie, I can't give you that information. I work for Quinn too; if he ever got wind of this…'

Scottie flicks up a contract. She types in a number. It floats on the screen between them. She grins. She points at it. 'What have you got to tell me that's worth this amount?'

Benny eyes the number. His mind races now, but the money is everything to him.

'Quinn said if we can get Henry back to his old vibrant self, he'll give him management of the new project.'

'What new project?'

'Scottie…'

'What project?' She pokes a finger at the number on her screen. 'This is a taster number, Benny. Do you understand? If you do right by me, there'll be a ton more of it, okay? Tell me, what new project?'

'A kind of human-services city, run by robots.'

'How far along is it?'

'I don't know. They don't tell me. In planning, maybe? This stays between us, right?' At the thought of a confrontation with

Quinn, Benny's stomach turns. His voice becomes loud. 'Between us, right, Scott?'

'Benny, you can trust me more than you can trust yourself.' Scottie spins the screen to him. 'If you want the money, sign it.'

A sense that this has turned into Scottie's meeting has him shrinking back in his seat, but he lifts a finger and squiggles his name under the number.

'You're connected?'

Benny reaches behind his ear and touches a finger to his dots. Scottie flings the contract to him. His dots vibrate, and the deal is done. It's already done. His eyes begin to water.

Scottie shrugs at him. 'Now that wasn't too hard, was it?'

4

Henry & Vince

Henry thuds his fist on Vince's front door then rests his forehead against it, gently. There's no sign of movement from inside. It's at this moment, every time; it waits for Henry at this door—the sense of unease, that all is not okay. He presses the lock code into the keypad and pushes the door inward. The stale air engulfs him.

'In here!' Vince calls from the back room, startling Henry.

Henry picks a pathway through the loungeroom, which is thick with hoarded boxes of junk. There are stacks of Data Traps that have been pulled from self-drives, there are piles of clothes and there's an enormous cardboard box with a mountain of bubble wrap. A motorcycle with its parts strewn across the floor takes up most of the space against the wall. Henry crouches down, tears off a small square of bubble wrap and presses his thumb to a bubble, rolling it between his fingers, then squeezes a pop out of it. It's the big kind; inch-sized bubbles that shimmy under his fingers. He pockets it and follows Vince's voice to the half-closed door of the bedroom.

'I'm coming in,' Henry warns.

Vince has no shame when it comes to displays of wobbly nakedness, and Henry has no desire to witness that—again.

'Come in, my friend,' Vince calls.

Vince is possibly Henry's closest friend, and he's an oddball. He speaks in phrases as though he's on a stage: 'We leave now,' or 'This way, my friend.'

Henry pushes the door inward. It moves a few inches, then butts up against more of Vince's junk. Henry curls his head around the door; piles of clothes, biscuit wrappers, books, corn-chip packs and travel bags stuffed full of who knows what press against the door. 'One day, I'll come in here, and you'll be squashed under all this junk, and you won't ever find your way out again.'

'Or,' replies Vince, 'I'll live happily ever after among all my favourite possessions.'

Vince is sitting up, alert, in the middle of his king-sized bed. He's surrounded by screens: phone, touchpad, and an open hologram which fades in and out with the poor connection to the public web. Notes are sprawled across them all.

Henry puts his shoulder to the door and pushes. 'What's this?' He gestures at the devices on the bed. He knows what it is. It's always the same, but he likes to give the idea air for discussion.

'A new claim to put to that dodgy hospital.' Vince taps the touchpad, his fingernail clicking on the screen. In front of him on the bed is a plate with toast crusts that give off a faint scent of Vegemite. An empty coffee cup sits on it and clunks with every slight movement of the bed. Four more mugs rest on the bedside table, with various stages of mould dotting the rims.

'I'm surprised they still take your calls.'

'I'm after funds for a new chair, and you know what? I want a nice one this time. A really nice one with wide wheels, stair climbers, underwater options—'

'Underwater? That's a thing?'

'Yes, it's a thing—for water aerobics or swimming. I need it, I want it and I shall have it, and then you'll stop complaining about me never going anywhere. I'll roll right into the ocean like a little baby turtle.'

Henry scans the room to find a place to sit. Vince's eyes follow him, amused. This lift in Vince's spirits is unexpected, but good. He finds a clear spot on the corner of the bed and positions himself on the edge of the slippery bed covers, with his feet firm on the floor.

'I'll modernise with whatever money I can squeeze out of them.' Vince throws his touchpad at him. 'Look at this.' The screenshot is of a wheelchair, which he's circled. It's modern, and the facets and add-ons are signalled with big clouds of thought bubbles.

'Nice,' says Henry.

'I'm far from done with that hospital.' Vince grabs the touchpad and slides through the pages. 'Take a look at this,' he says, tossing it back to Henry. 'Page seven.'

Henry glances through the article without speaking.

'It's another outbreak,' Vince says. 'They've closed that ward down again—the same ward I stayed in. The same ward they gave the all-clear to last year.'

Henry tosses the touchpad onto the bed. 'This story's not about you though, is it?'

'No, but they want the story to go away, and they'll be looking to pay off troublemakers. That's me—troublemaker.' He points at his smiling cheeks. 'And I won't go away until I get what I'm owed. The least I can force them to do is placate me with cash, and the most I can force them to do is take a serious look at their bug epidemic.'

Vince smiles, but his skin has taken on the sallow look that it does when he speaks about the hospital. He behaves as if this pushing for compensation is a fun game, but there may never be an end to it.

'You could sell your motorbike and buy the new chair with the money. It takes up a lot of space, and you don't need a reminder like that in your face every day.'

'Leave the bike alone. I like seeing it; it gives me hope. I'll be riding it again, some day. The accident put me in hospital, but it's the hospital-bred infection that took my legs. It's not the bike's fault.'

Vince is upbeat and positive today, but Henry knows that once he shuts the front door, Vince goes into combat with the silence. Henry turns words over in his thoughts, looking for the most sensitive way to suggest Vince should take up the spare room in Henry's apartment again. He picks up a booklet that's been discarded on the floor. 'Have you thought about this info on Scottie Fuennel? Did you read it?'

Vince takes the booklet from him and tosses it across the room. 'I appreciate it, Henry, but it's not for me.'

'They do amazing things over at Scottie's. Her cyborg technology is superior, and it's humane—people-focussed, you know?'

'You surprise me, Henry. You of all people—the vintage guy pushing the plastic limbs. I'm not interested in fake toes. I'm real, Henry—every inch of me. When you look at me, you really are looking at me. The real deal.' He thumps his chest with his fist. 'Look at this.' He passes back the touchpad to Henry, with an open email displayed. 'They threatened to cut my pension if I don't show my face down there. You got time for a cruise around town tomorrow? Help me give them an earful?' Vince moves out of the bed and perches on the end, beside Henry.

'Nice change of subject, Vincey. I can take you to the city now, if you like? I've got an intern to pick up at the station.'

As Henry speaks, his attention is drawn to a swelling movement of the covers on the other side of the bed, and, in that moment, there emerges—like Gulliver from ropes—a pale face that, as the sheets slip away to the floor, gradually reveals itself to be the head, then the neck, and then the body of a woman.

Vince's eyes follow Henry's gaze. 'Have you not met Greta?' he asks, and he casually throws a thumb over his shoulder. Vince smiles because, of course, Henry has not met Greta. Greta is new.

'Nope, I'm inclined to say I haven't met Greta. And here I was thinking the piles of bubble wrap in the lounge were a new exercise machine.'

'It is kind of a new exercise machine.' Vince grins.

Vince grabs a plate as it begins to slide from the covers with the emergence of his bed companion, who has been so still and quiet this whole time that Henry suspects Vince intended to keep this new thing in his life hidden.

It's a serene face that smiles at Henry, but her eyes dart down, up, down, then up again as it takes in the details of what it means to be Henry.

'Hello Henry,' it says. 'Lovely to see you again.'

Although Henry has worked for Quinn for many years, he doesn't deal with the social bots. It's not his job. His focus is the business of getting contracts signed, deliveries delivered and debts paid. In fact, he prefers not to think about the bots as functioning beings and how they're used, at all.

Vince watches Henry's face.

'We've met before?' Henry asks it.

'Not exactly,' it says, 'but I've been aware of you.'

And now Henry finds that, apart from complete surprise, he's feeling agitated by the idea of it knowing him, but he not knowing it, and the only way he can manage to express an opinion is to mock Vince: 'What were you just saying about being the real deal?' Henry says, and he thumps his fist against his own chest.

5

Dale & Scottie

The train careens to the left, and Dale's stomach rushes with it, out across the suburbs, and then settles again as the train pulls back and straightens up, tight and hard. Dale's glad to have a six-seater to herself. She's certain the worry over what she's got herself into is showing in her face.

After three, long hours, the train slows and moves painstakingly through the city's platforms then drifts to a halt at her stop. As she steps from the train, the wind rushes through the station and sends cold air through her clothing. A thrum of drones congregates in the air above her. Swarming like bees, they hum and buffet against each other. Where she's from, drones draw attention. They're singular, fascinating, even considered delightful. They're not this black mass of menace. She'd like to change her mind, and get on the next train home, but it's way too late for that.

Nearby, a woman dressed in muted tones of beiges and browns waves a drone down with her phone. Dale smiles at her; she modelled herself on this very style of woman. At the drone's double-tone, ting-tong sound of the lock, the woman takes her coffee from it and a small parcel too; maybe it's a pastry or a tart. Dale imagines it has strawberry jam, as though it's for her, as if the comfort of jam would make today easier. The drone ascends. It's red-and-black signage flashes, and then it's gone. A dot among dots. The redbacks of the sky.

A boy hurries past. He shoves Dale with his school bag, grazing her arm as he leaps and catches a train already in motion. She side-steps an oncoming stream of travellers and wobbles on her new high heels. A rash of blood forms on her grazed arm.

People pause around her to look at their phones and tap their dots. She takes short breaths to avoid the wafting dust from the trains. She looks around for a sign with her name on it. The plan was that somebody would be here to meet her. She had laid it out neatly in her mind, but they're nowhere to be seen, and this wrinkle in the plan nudges at her confidence.

She embarked on this venture four weeks ago with the creation of a persona, one completely at odds with her own, allowing her to be the person she needs to be. But now, she's rattled. She bolsters herself by reciting the list of attributes she had decided to take on: unflappable, uncaring, straightforward, daring—I don't give a fuck. A personality to wear like a cloak.

She pulls her bag close against her legs. A woman heads toward her, her face focussed, and then moves on past while hurrying along her four small jiggling children—a family size that must be a pleasant throwback to the last government. The crowd thins. The trains become still. A fake vintage clock echoes throughout the station with a confected tick thunk, tick thunk, tick thunk, and the vast building pulsates with the emptiness.

Her phone vibrates in her pocket, and she takes it out. It's Esther from QRC. She breathes in. It rings and rings. She breathes out. Train noise builds around her. Heels click, and the drones return to hover. The energised air needles her anxiety.

She brings the phone to her ear. 'Dale speaking.'

A voice squeaks at her.

'I can't hear you,' Dale says. Announcements bark over the loud-speaker: platforms and times and trains. '*Esther?*' she shouts, and she walks until she finds a quiet alcove.

'*Dale,*' Esther shouts back through the phone, '*It's Esther from QRC. Henry will be late. He'll swing by the bus terminal in a yellow Mini soon. Can you get there?*'

'Thanks for the call, Esther; walking as we speak.'

The phone goes dead.

Dale is pretty certain it's the first time she's ever said 'walking as we speak'. She hangs up and does not walk as she speaks. Her steps falter at this term she's pulled straight out of a movie. Today, and over the next few months, she'll be drawing on anything from any-where to become this somebody she is not, and the recent memory of the last time she was, mistakenly, so sure of herself begins to tinker about in the background of her thoughts, chipping away at her confidence.

≈

To be fair, it was a positive sign that she'd been invited to an interview. The bright, white walls at the Family Growth Centre screamed success and filled her with the belief that she'd have no trouble getting approval. The interviewer was casual, pleasant, and made a joke about signing her up for sleep counselling, and then she sent Dale multiple files to guide her through the process of becoming a new mother.

Dale left the meeting with an urge to share the news with every-one she passed. She strode along the street and gazed at the clear sky. She bumped into a woman. Dale's apology was all about herself:

'I'm sorry. I've got good news. I'm having a baby, so sorry.' She felt overwhelmed by the sense of being at the beginning of an exciting, and positive, change in her life.

Dale was unprepared for the letter of denial. Her timing had been bad. With strong religion now having a moment, the right-wing government had made the decision to ride this wave of righteousness by flexing its power over family-planning laws and clamping down on singles starting a family. It pinged in her dots before she arrived home that day. She glanced at the subject line, 'Family Initiation Application', but didn't read it. This was how sure she'd been of the outcome of her application. She tossed around ideas for names—Ava, Lena, maybe Winnie? With black hair or brown. Green eyes, maybe freckles?

The disappointment when it came was hard to accept, as though her body had prepared for the idea of a baby, and then felt the loss. Her muscles ached. She felt exhausted. The strangeness of her reaction frightened her. She'd been denied what the previous government had led her to believe was possible. In her mind, she had already been there—a happy family of two.

She reacted to this injustice by searching for a way to retaliate, and when she found what she needed to ease the disappointment, it felt like sliding into cool water on a blistering hot day. She slid easily into Scottie Fennel's Community Core; a cause in which to place her anger, and a place to fight against laws that have forgotten humanity.

≈

Dale thrusts down the handle on her bag and releases the long arm to tug it along behind her. In moments like these that her mind wanders, an unhelpful vulnerability sets in. She digs deep to find anger and lures her confidence back. These ridiculous laws are political, and they can and will be changed. She steps aside to let a stream of pedestrians go by, and then pulls out her phone and makes a call.

Scottie picks up, but Dale speaks first: 'He's late, Scottie. So much for Mr Hotshot Efficiency.' The tremor in her own voice surprises her. She takes in a slow breath.

'Take it as a sign he has his priorities straight,' Scottie answers bluntly. 'You need to remember you're not his priority.'

Hearing Scottie's reprimand, her face reddens at what she realises is her need for reassurance. Communication from her to The Core is supposed to be limited, and she sees the need to muster a show of confidence now.

'I'm standing here on the curb in the dusty heat, waiting for a guy who's an hour late. Yeah, I understand I'm not his priority.'

'You're an intern, you'll need to work hard to—'

'Yes, Scottie, I will. I'll gain his trust.'

'You're a champ, Dale. I'll see you soon.'

It was an unnecessary phone call. She won't call Scottie again without good reason. Her display of unease has shown her to be erratic, which isn't an ideal attribute for the job. She imagines getting back on the train and going straight back home. She could settle into her cosy couch, maybe binge on a series or two. She sets down her bag and sits on it. She takes out her phone and looks at her socials. They're all fake, just like her new persona is fake. She has an urge to message a real friend, but it'd be the beginning of the end of this, and she'd never forgive herself for giving up this opportunity to help shape the world into one she'd prefer to live in. Besides, she's certain her old boss won't take apologies in return for her old job back.

She picks up her bag handle and pulls the bag behind her toward the bus terminal. She sets it down in the shade of a bus and keeps an eye out on the streets for Henry King and his Mini. She thinks about Henry, the robot guy, driving a petrol-driven rust bucket of all things, and she smiles and feels her confidence returning.

Across the main circuit, a self-drive fails to slow at the backed-up afternoon traffic. Presumably calculating the situation and making the decision to divert, sliding swiftly up the gutter and onto the footpath—and it strikes a woman, sending her into the air to land hard on the road. It's over in seconds, and Dale is moving off the curb and across the street to kneel at the woman's side before she realises she's drawn attention to herself. The pedestrian raises a hand and touches Dale's arm to indicate she's okay.

Dale needs to remove herself from this situation, but she stays with the woman while the crowd grows. Within minutes medics arrive and take over the situation. Dale falls back into the crowd. She catches a glimpse of the yellow Mini at the bus terminal. It's sporting a large bumper-band all the way around the car—either Henry King is a terrible driver or he doesn't trust anyone else on the road.

She makes her way toward Henry. The door to his car doesn't open with the first tug. She gives it a yank, and the handle comes away in her hand. She crouches down to the low window and peers inside. Henry leans across to look up at her. His dopey smile forgives her for the broken handle, and with a push, he opens the door for her. She makes herself small, hunched and rounded to climb in under his gaze. She untangles the floppy seatbelt and fastens herself in.

Behind them, a bus honks twice. She's heard so much about Henry King—what a professional he is, what a slick businessman and what a sharp talker; *be careful of Henry King*. She's been warned about his wit and cunning, but here he is in a shit car, late, with a brown stain on his pants that she hopes is coffee, and seeming to struggle to form a sentence. She's relieved. He's their access to

QRC—the prized target. Sadly, for him, it's looking easy. She shifts in the worn seat until she's comfortable. She could almost feel sorry for him—almost.

She pokes her hand out to him. 'Dale,' she says.

6

Quinn & Benny

Quinn's chin rests on his fist, propped up by his thick elbow. He considers these little chats with Benny to be a kind of morning refresher, a change of pace before he dives into the muck of his day. Benny's view of the world is unpredictable, and it serves as a reminder that there's always another way of looking at things, albeit from an odd angle. He picks a chunk from his morning muffin, pokes it into his large mouth and chews hard in defiance of his doctor's pleadings about his health. His head bounces rhythmically on his fist with each quick bite.

Benny's face, with his puppy-dog eyes, nods back at him after every few words, and gives away his every thought with big, excited eyes. Quinn has respect for Benny—not immense respect, but enough to keep him around. He's a nice enough boy, which is a failing in business, but nonetheless, it seems to work for him.

'And I'll tell you another thing,' Benny continues, 'she employs women exclusively. What do you think about that? I understand she's making a point, but she *is* actually running a business, right? This isn't politics, Quinn; this is life.'

Quinn understands Benny's loyalty is opportunistic, and he's certain Scottie will receive the same monologue from Benny—if she hasn't already—only in reverse; it'll be all about what Benny can do for Scottie, exclusively. However, Benny is diligent in his work and usually delivers on what he claims he'll do—and that's a big tick for him. He's meticulous in his personal life, which is unnecessary but fascinating. Quinn studies his face. He's never completely understood Benny. His hair angles across his eyes like a crooked curtain, cut sharp. His lips, painted burgundy like wine, frame his teeth—teeth so bleached that Quinn can make out the blood-filled nerves suspended like mini nooses inside them. Benny's attention to appearance screams insecurity.

All of this is exactly the way Quinn loves Benny to be: a fragile boy with an intense desire to please. Quinn slides his desk drawer open and takes out an image of Benny. He reaches through Benny's gram and pins the portrait to the office wall, alongside the other images of staff.

'I'm not sure that's entirely true, Benny. I think you'll find plenty of male employees over there at Scottie's joint. But I take your point, she's heavy on women—it's kind of her thing, isn't it.'

Benny is the employee Quinn likes to keep hidden. He keeps him for the unsavoury jobs, and Benny's willingness to take these jobs on has Quinn turning a blind eye to his tendency to say— and do— all the wrong things at the wrong time, every time. He's the black sheep, the oddball who doesn't quite belong anywhere, but he has endless uses.

'I mean, she claims she's all about equality, but it's a bit sexist, isn't it, Quinn?'

'Well, I've heard her say that men and women approach robotics differently, and frankly, it's actually one point we agree on.'

Quinn takes a dart from the box on his desk and holds the silver rod between his thumb and finger. The cold metal is refreshing on his skin. In his world of weightless plastics, the cold, heavy steel grounds him in the way a sharp prick brings focus to thoughts. He pulls his hand back near his ear, takes aim and throws. It slides through the gram, misses the photo of Benny and hits the portrait of Henry in the left nostril.

'But I didn't call to talk about Scottie.' Benny pauses, perhaps expecting Quinn to ask what it is he has called for.

It allows Quinn time to pivot the conversation to Henry and encourage Benny to focus his talents for wrongdoing on the company, rather than on his shaky business ideas. 'Tell me about Henry and his mental health,' Quinn enquires.

'Henry? He won't take my calls. He's avoiding me, but I think—'

'Henry is our guy; remember that, Benny.'

'So you've said,' Benny replies, bluntly.

Benny's envious nature entertains Quinn, and that's saying something as Quinn is a person rarely amused. His life revolves around the entertainment business, through the creation of technology for pleasure—from handheld plastic gadgets all the way up to the highest quality social bots that be and do any damn thing his clients want them to—but it's human nature and human failings that amuse Quinn. He loves slapstick: the old kind, Charlie Chaplain, Laurel and Hardy, and The Marx Brothers. Quinn's wind-down time in the evening is alone, in his home cinema, with black-and-white movies.

Quinn tugs the dart out of Henry's nostril. He touches a finger to the hole he's made, pressing the paper back down, and smooths out the nose. 'I want Henry back in shape; right now, he's unreliable. This self-pity thing he's got going on makes me uneasy. He's not in a dependable state of mind, and he's incapable of taking on new work like Project City. He needs a shake-up. Does he need a holiday, do you think?'

Quinn hears Benny suck in a wheezy breath to speak.

'And no, Benny, you can't do the job. I need a guy with experience in how I work. Just between you and me, I need someone I can trust. Most don't get us; they can't hack the way we work. They come in, I train them up, I get them to the point where I can let them in on a job, and they baulk, get all virtuous and leave. We need a guy who has longevity with the company—a hired gun we can trust, you get me?'

Quinn would like to be honest with Benny and tell him that he just doesn't have the class to manage an entire city of robots, but honesty doesn't work with Benny. He doesn't take criticism too well. To tell him he has no class would be way too much of an insult for the sensitive man-boy.

'I'd do you well in that position, Quinn; you know I would.'

Poor Benny. There's such sadness in his voice; he's so emotional.

'I won't lie to you, Benn, Henry needs this job. He's worked under me for long enough. It's time we brought him into the light. He needs the responsibility. You understand? It's your job to get him back into shape for us all. He needs you to do this for him. *I* need you to do this for him. This is where you do your best work.'

'He'll come good,' Benny says, 'I guarantee it. I have plans. And speaking of plans, Quinn, I have great news for us. Listen to this: I secured a commitment from Scottie to invest in the club.'

Quinn throws the dart again and spears Benny's portrait in his plump, purple lips. Never in a million years did he expect Scottie to come to the party on one of Benny's hair-brained ideas. Has he missed some kind of value in it?

Benny squirms, waiting for an answer, while Quinn wrangles his thoughts around one.

'Henry needs you to give your full attention to his health, so I'm not sure that extending yourself to big ideas like this club will help anybody here. Don't spread yourself too thin, Benny. You get what I'm saying? Don't let it distract you from our day-to-day projects. That's what brings the dollars in.'

Quinn throws another dart, hard, and it hits the image of Esther —his only female employee—in the neck. He needs to remedy that, but it's difficult to find women with a positive opinion of social bots. He made a point of bringing female interns into the six-month team, but he struck gold with Esther. She's the best kind of female: she thinks like a man, is aggressive, never cackles, but is female. Tick. And she doesn't mind a doll; in fact, she owns a loony one of the Berthas, which is unexpected, but excellent. Esther's existence is good value when he needs to make the feminist equality point.

Benny turns his head away, off screen, and mumbles.

'Who's there with you, Benny? Are we keeping this private?'

'Sure. Nobody here but me and the cat. Quinn, you're a man who can recognise a great start-up when he sees one; that's why you gave me your word. You said if I could get Scottie on board, you'd come on board with her. You said this. I'd go as far as saying that choosing to ignore my club is a big mistake, but I'm sure you'd be knowing this already.'

'Mistake?' Quinn moves his chair forward and takes hold of the dart in Esther's neck. He pulls, and it becomes a gash in her throat.

Benny breathes heavily through the gram at the possibility of not clinching Quinn's investment after all.

It occurs to Quinn, for the very first time, that he thinks of Benny as a kind of stupid son. Benny's dedication has been solid from day one, like he hopes a son's would be. If Benny had smarts in business, he'd give him more responsibility, in fact he'd give him the entire company, eventually. but he doesn't, so he won't. 'I tell you what—you go ahead, map out a business plan and see what you can shake up, then we'll run it by accounting and—'

'Put it this way, we'll kill two birds here, Quinn. We're sitting on a gold mine.'

Quinn lets a snort escape. 'What birds shall we kill, and where is this gold mine, Benny?'

'Henry is the bird. I can heal his Little Problem and put The Uncanny Valley Club in motion at the same time, and in case you haven't realised it yet, the club is our gold mine. It's a win-win for you, Quinn. If you back this idea, I'll consider any suggestions for improvement from you. I'll consider shares, and maybe even a partnership down the track? Put your spin on it—whatever takes your fancy—and at the same time, put the money into your best guy. I'm talking Henry here, not me.'

Win-win for you, Quinn. Quinn likes the sound of that. 'Have Henry trial your club? You're a smooth talker—I'll give you that, Benn—but Henry won't be fooled into that. He may be bored with himself right now, but he's not stupid.'

'You're not hearing me, Quinn. We both know Henry won't go for that. I'm not here to tell you how to do your job, of course, but this is what you should do: you ask him to look the club over for you to see if it's worth the investment, and while he's in the club, I'll give him the royal treatment. He'll love it. You have no idea, Quinn. Have you seen the European clubs? He'll love it. You'll love it. For fuck's sake, we'll all love it. You think he needs a holiday? This is better than a trip to the beach. Let's bury him in The Uncanny Valley Club experience, and I guarantee you'll have your old Henry back. We'll razz him up good 'n' proper. All he needs is a good going over from one of your best girls. You know what his problem is, right?'

'I've heard the story.'

'Let's have him try out a new model. A man like you, I bet you've got an awesome new model in the works.'

'You've got me interested, Benny—I'll give you that.' Quinn pokes at Benny's nose on the gram. 'Tell me this: how much will Scottie put in? Put me down to equal Scottie.'

'Great, but Quinn, I do need money, but I also need dolls. This is not an experiment; it's the real deal. You give me the dolls, and I'll get a start this same day. I have big plans for this. It'll be a glorious venue, but glory costs more than I have in my pocket. You'd be knowing this fact already, with you being a fan of glory yourself.'

Quinn laughs. It's not the flattery that amuses him, but that Benny believes flattery works. It probably does work on his clients. 'What say I inject a trickle of resources, a fleet of bots to rent for your club experiment, so I can get a squiz at what you plan to do with it. You know what a trickle means, don't you? A basic fleet, Benny. And I want updates, or I'll be forced to repossess them, and I don't want to have to do that to you, Benny, do I.'

Benny jigs, his elbows out like chicken wings and his knees up, on his plush, blue carpet. His stomach bounces up, and down and all over the gram.

'And for doing this for you, Benny, you'll make good on your promise. You'll get Henry back to his old self. He's your priority. I don't care if he's in therapy every day of the week. I won't spend another ten years trying to find a gun I can trust with our new city.'

Benny's face becomes sombre, and his excitement settles. He doesn't fool Quinn. Benny doesn't do sombre. Time will prove his capabilities with this job.

'There's no doubt I'll have Henry in perfect shape, and you'll get your updates,' Benny agrees.

'Okay, Benny, we're done here. You'll be seeing your new pieces ready for pick up at the warehouse today.'

Quinn flicks a hand up through the gram and hangs up on Benny's open mouth, which is no doubt on the verge of a mono-logue of appreciation. His flapping lips vanish. The wall of torn portraits glares back at Quinn. The room is quiet now Benny's bustle of personality has left the space. Quinn looks at his phone. His finger hovers over Scottie's face, but what would he say? 'What's your game? This isn't your thing.' Better she doesn't know he's already chasing her on it.

The security monitors lining his office walls are motion-free. Not one employee is at their desk yet. Quinn flashes the time with a shake of his wrist: 7:10. He wants to see Henry at his desk. He wants to see the face of the guy he handed to Benny, of all people, to play with like a wind-up toy.

7
——

Scottie & Henry

Scottie ended the call from Dale, who was milling about at the train station, abruptly. Dale had a shaky tone in her voice that she really needs to get a hold of. If she doesn't show some chutzpah, they may need to ask her to move on—Quinn and his crew don't give two shits about anyone but themselves, and they won't be kind to her. Scottie's phone now buzzes with a number she doesn't recognise. With Dale still in her thoughts, she lets the call go to voicemail.

Scottie turns her plants around, one by one, to show their dark sides to the morning sunlight. With little metal scissors, she snips at her herbs, a leaf of mint, a petal of marigold, a snip of Brahmi, a leaf of sage. The crushed scents are strong. She rests them on her tongue, stretches out her legs and gazes out the window.

The grotesque high-rises blink their reflective walls at her, and traffic grids hum and block the sky. In the six years she's owned this building, the town has transformed dramatically. The council have made inroads toward cooling the city, planting evergreen trees with large canopies that line the streets; encouraging greenery-covered rooftops and angled walls; enforcing constraints on concrete; and incentivising businesses to prioritise solar windows in new buildings. Restaurants within the city walls are limited to vegetarian and entomophagous meals, new families are legally restricted to no more than two children, and no single person can initiate a family; this last law is contentious to many in The Core, but it's one that Scottie happens to agree with. And still, the view from her window has her pining for genuine forestry.

Quinn owns most of the buildings that surround hers. Her aim in moving her business here was to show the world the useful and humane work done through cyborg enhancement at Fuennel Industries, and at the same time, make a dent in the growth of social robots that collect an obscene amount of money for Quinn. She'd hoped to be a significant problem to Quinn and shine a light on his failings, but his work continues to thrive. To make an impact, Scottie has made the decision to be loud, to be organised and brutal, and to hit Quinn where it hurts—right in his money bags.

Thalia knocks on Scottie's door and pops her head in. 'You wanted to see me?'

'Just for a second, Thalia. I want to see that face of yours and know you're okay.'

Thalia stays beyond the doorway. 'Okay? I'm fine.'

'Come in and sit a while.' Scottie waves her in.

Thalia's face remains serious as she enters and sits down.

'Tell me you're okay about the restructured activist group,' Scottie requests. As a member from the beginning (Scottie once related to her as her partner, but has realised Thalia has incrementally been withdrawing), Thalia is the one person she doesn't want to lose from The Core. She's given her room to move within the extremes, and she really hopes Thalia will get comfortable with the new ways, sooner rather than later.

'I'm okay with it; I'm fine.' Thalia's eyes move around the room, gazing everywhere but at Scottie, and come to rest on the little plants.

'You need to understand that the work The Core has done has made us visible; we have a presence, but it's not enough. People who take note of us are already supporters. I know it goes against our nature, but activism is the next step. We need to become a disrupter.'

'Of course. I'm removing myself from the violent protests, but other than that, I'm right behind you, as always—all the way. You don't need to call me in to know that.'

Part of Scottie's new strategy will mean knowing who will go the distance with her, and who of her people will commit no matter the consequence. Her old strategy made room for everybody to set their own level of participation, which felt more like a hippie commune than an organised business. 'Will you come to the next meeting? I won't ask you to play a big part. Just be a face at the gathering and stand with me. More like a prop really.' Scottie laughs. 'We have a lot of new members, and I need a show of familiar faces. Is that good with you?'

'I'll be there'

Scottie smiles. 'That's all I want to know.'

Thalia rises to leave.

'Wait. We've been in this together from the start, so I expect it's important to you to keep up to date with who's joined us and where we're at with everything. You still want to be kept in the loop?'

Thalia rests one hand on the doorknob. 'We've been over this, Scottie. You have my loyalty if you need it, so let's leave it at that.'

Scottie's frustration with Thalia for distancing herself has become difficult to keep in check. Scottie takes in a deep breath. 'As The Core changes in tactics, clarity is really important. We can't have some of us waving swords while others wave flags.'

Thalia's eyes widen momentarily at the word 'swords'.

'Metaphorical swords,' Scottie clarifies. 'I want us to be in agreement about the new direction.'

'Let me be clear, Scottie.' Thalia edges back in the doorway a little. 'We can't keep having these spontaneous little meetings where you tell me how you want things to be, and at the same time you don't accept what I'm telling you. Unless you agree with me that The Core is a peaceful organisation, which—in case you've forgotten—was our intention when we sat in your car four years ago and decided to take action against the robotics industry, then I have to remove myself slightly. I'm still here; I'm just not'—Thalia mockingly whips her arm through the air, left and right, as though brandishing a sword—'an active vigilante.'

'Vigilante?' Scottie laughs. 'I don't think we're that. We were naïve, Thalia. We thought that simply existing would be enough to curb Quinn's progress. We thought the community would look at us and see that our way is better, but they don't see the long-term damage Quinn does with his mindless production-line of sex bots. All they see is a short-term fascination and thrill. Nobody will pay attention to us unless we're loud about it.'

'Be loud then, but ask yourself this: do you need to hurt people? That's not who we are; at least, that's not who we were. If you publicly claim these acts of violence, people will judge you harshly. Does the thought of that make you happy?'

Scottie is floored at how easy it is for Thalia to walk away from everything they worked for. 'I've taken on board your concerns, Thalia, I really have, but our old ways didn't do anything for us. Being timid and meekly pointing out our views achieves nothing. After we claim these acts, we'll have the attention we need, and then we'll have an opportunity to explain to the world why we've done these things. It's only then that people will listen to what we have to say about Quinn. The bigger and bolder our actions, the more attention we'll garner.'

Scottie's phone rings again. She glances at it.

'We'll agree to disagree then,' Thalia concludes. Then she slips out the door and shuts it behind her. She can't get out of Scottie's office quick enough.

Scottie's phone buzzes and buzzes with the unknown number. She slides it on and brings it to her ear. 'Yes?'

'Scottie?'

'Yes?'

'It's Henry.'

'Henry King?' Scottie's mind is still on Thalia, and her eyes are on the closed door. The unexpected call from Quinn's right-hand guy requires a moment to shift tact.

'Hi Scottie, got time for a chat?'

Scottie leans back in her chair and looks to the ceiling. 'Henry, this is a surprise.'

'I imagine it is, but ... I won't take up much of your time. I've been contemplating making this call to you ... You can understand I'm hesitant, but I'm calling to ask for your expertise. I have a friend in need of your work—your cyborg program. I really think you could improve his life.'

Henry has slipped so easily into a natural conversation that Scottie wonders if she's missed something. 'Henry, I'm sorry, this isn't a service that you can call up like a pizza. There's a process to follow. I'll give you the number for our psychologist's office. Get your friend to call there.'

'Scottie, let me explain. I'd like to bypass the usual avenues, if I could? I want to come in through the back door, so to speak.'

Scottie remains silent in her thoughts.

'And can I remind you a little bit of our history together,' he continues, 'can I call in my IOU?' Henry laughs nervously.

Scottie laughs too. It's the only suitable response to his reminder of how badly she failed at life back then. That she called in favours from everybody she knew is her biggest regret that seems to follow her everywhere she goes. They're different people now, but she can recall things about Henry that he, too, would be happy to bury. Still, even with their history, this is an unwelcome request. 'Let me explain my point of view to you,' she says. 'The question I'm asking myself is this: can I trust you? I can't let you walk into our services as if you're an average client, can I?'

'I guess you can't take my word for it, but of course you can trust me. I hope you can think of me, in this instance, as just me, Henry. Not an employee of QRC.'

Scottie laughs again to buy herself time to think. Henry King has laid himself at her feet, and that right there is an occasion to take advantage of. 'Henry, how can I word this so that you understand. This is what I'm thinking: if I allow this favour to you, can I protect my company from all the ways you might take advantage of my opening Fuennel Industries doors up to you? I get that you're after personal care for your friend, but I think it'd be better for us both if you step back and let your friend do this on his own, through the proper channels, and keep our working relationship out of it.'

'Scottie, I know you can help him, but he needs a push. He won't come without me dragging him in. He thinks of enhancement as unnatural. He believes he won't be human if he undergoes enhancement. He doesn't fully understand it as we do. He needs to be convinced.'

Scottie tries to read between the lines of everything Henry has to say, but it seems Henry is being honest. 'I'll give you some advice, Henry. Some people have to help themselves before you can help them. It's your friend's choice. He shouldn't be forced. If he wants to go through with it, I can help him—that's easy—but I won't let *you* anywhere near Fuennel Industries.'

'I wouldn't be too concerned, Scottie. If we wanted access to Fuennel Industries, it wouldn't be hard. In fact, I'm sure we already have. I'm trying to be honest with you here. Listen, I can't take him elsewhere; nobody will bother with his salty arse. I'm asking you to take the time to talk to my friend and explain to him what's possible. Scottie, let me put it this way, what can *I* do for *you* to make this happen?'

'There you go; that's what I want to hear.' Scottie raps a knuckle on the desk. 'This is what I know about you, Henry: you have a problem, and I—'

'No. I don't have a problem.'

'You sign up too, and have your problem examined, along with your friend, and we have a deal.'

Henry groans. 'What do you want with me?'

'I want to help you, that's all, and at the same time, maybe I can educate you. Maybe I can bring you into the fold—the better one.' Scottie smiles to herself. 'Do we have a deal, Henry?'

'I can't. My problem is in the past; there's nothing to see here. It's not a part of this transaction.'

'Okay, I'm sorry then. If you can't put yourself on the line, then I can't trust you and I can't help you.'

Henry answers with silence.

Scottie doesn't have time to wait for Henry King to decide what is more important: his friend's needs or his own dignity.

'If you want to help your friend, give our psychologist a call and book yourself in.' Scottie hangs up. She plucks a bunch of marigold flowers, drops them in a teapot and sets the water heater on. It doesn't matter. If Henry arrives at the door, great; if he doesn't, nothing's lost—she still has Benny gathering video of Henry. Poor Henry will be her guinea pig no matter which way he goes.

8

Henry, Dale & Vince

The chemical scent of new train upholstery comes into the car with her. Henry lets go of Dale's outstretched hand and presses his hand in his pocket to touch an antiseptic wipe. She tugs the seatbelt until it unravels, then shoves it into the lock again and again and again, until it finds its place and snaps in. She shifts uncomfortably in the seat. He touches a finger to the steering wheel, waits for her to settle, then pumps the accelerator, pulls on the choke and turns the key in the ignition.

When he pulled into the bus terminal earlier, he peered through his small windows to look for an anxious intern. She was nowhere in sight. And now, here she is, fresh from heroism—the woman who tended the toppled pedestrian.

Vince's music still fills the car. Henry switches it off.

He notices her eyes look up to the elevation cars. After living in the city for years now, he takes for granted the upper tiers sweeping in circles around the outskirts of the city, and the free flow of elevation cars wafting about like boats in the wide drive-space.

'Where are you from?' he asks.

'Central country. We're a bit backward there.' She laughs. 'We've only just gone completely electric, and our mayor's still fighting turbine protests.'

The bus behind gives them a blast on the horn. After a stream of self-drives moves through the street, a gap opens in the traffic. Henry's phone buzzes in the console; it's a message from Vince: 'Ready'.

'I've got an errand to run,' he says. 'Do you need to get settled where you're staying, or shall we get straight to work?'

'Sure, let's go to work,' she replies. 'What are we doing?'

'It's pretty much watch and learn. You'll be fine.'

He glances at the door handle resting on the dusty floor. They travel in silence across the main road and swing around the circuit to pull up at the curb beside Vince. Vince taps on the passenger side window and wiggles his fingers at Dale.

'You'll need to climb into the back seat,' Henry tells her, 'or get out to let Vince in the back; your choice. Either way, there's no door handle now, so you'll need to open the door for him.'

Dale gets out of the car and pulls the chair forward for Vince. Henry climbs out too, folds Vince's wheelchair down and forces it into the boot. He squishes the door shut. Henry watches Vince and Dale banter inside the car, their heads nodding. Henry imagines the conversation:

'I'm Vince.'

'I'm Dale.'

'Cool.'

'Cool, cool, cool.'

She turns her head to look at Henry through the window, her eyes wide and red lips pressed together.

He climbs back in and closes his door gently. 'You'll be fine,' he says to her, 'You'll enjoy your time at QRC.' He drags a touchpad out from under his seat and hands it to her while he steers one-handedly into the street. 'Here, catch up on the details of the job.'

A sudden and violent jolt to the Mini sends Dale's head forward, cracking the dashboard as the car slides sideways across the road. She clasps her seat to steady herself, but it's over in a blink. She puts a palm to her forehead.

'Fuck me,' Vince says from the back seat, turning to look out of the window to see what struck them.

'I'm fine, I think,' Dale says, although nobody has spoken to her.

Henry takes a battered cap from the side pocket and tugs it on, pulling the beak low. He climbs out and circles the car, dragging a finger smoothly along the bumper-band. The bumbling self-drive has left a gold-tinted mark from where it rubbed. He peers in the self-drive's window. There are no passengers; it was most likely en route to a call. Henry opens its door, pulls down the data trap on the dash and tugs on it. Cars line up behind, blocked by the accident, honking in protest. He raises the back of his hand to them all, one finger extended. He pulls and thrashes at the data trap until the wires slide free.

'*I'll take that,*' Vince shouts through the window.

Once back in the car, Henry tosses it to him. Vince rolls it over and over in his hands, disappointed. He'll have wanted the whole data-trap box for his collection.

Dale looks at Vince through the rear-vision mirror. 'Do you erase the camera before you take the parts?'

Henry presses his foot to the accelerator and manoeuvres the car back into the street. The car tugging back with each change of gear. It's one of the many things he loves about the car: the control of the gears. They leave behind the honk of complaints and the self-drive, still and quiet, waiting for remote assistance. The street-vid will file them, but it'll be hard pressed to track Henry's car without the rego-chip of the modern cars.

Vince opens the data trap and pokes inside it, making interested noises. 'Uh-huh, yep.'

Dale points. 'That there… pull that bit out first, and there'll be less damage to the data trap.'

Henry smiles into the rear-vision mirror at Vince. Vince doesn't want the parts that most people do. He likes to watch data-trap footage.

'If we get caught, you can pay the tamper fine'—Vince laughs at Dale—'because you told me to do it.' But Vince will have no intention of tampering with it.

Dale touches a finger to her forehead, where it's already raised and blue.

'All good?' Henry asks.

'Think so,' she says.

'Headache?'

'Nope.'

'Backache?'

'Nope.'

'Let me know if you do.'

'Yup.'

'Good to work?'

'Yup.' Dale brings her lips together to make the 'p' pop: 'Yupp.'

'Have a glance at that file then.'

She slides through the file, casual but attentive. Vince hums to a strange, squeaky rap song, which has been switched on while Henry was out of the car. As they move south through the streets, the architecture changes from bright walls painted white with shining glass to dark boards and brick buildings with graffiti, and in various stages of neglect. Dale keeps her face in the file, focussed.

Henry pulls into a side street beside tall, weathered buildings with faded paintwork and aged to the point of falling apart fretwork. Graffiti colours every wall, all pointing to one theme: #NotInOurTown, #Resist, #NoRobotBrothels #NoSexRobots. Scottie Fuennel's Community Core is clearly active down here, and its members apparently know already what's coming to this end of town, way before Henry has been included in the discussion—with Quinn only letting it slip today that Benny intends to make a go of something here.

Henry's seat tilts as Vince leans into the front and pokes his head between them. 'Stop in the pub for a beer, hey?'

'There's no beer here, Vince; not a drop. These businesses have all been closed down.' Henry looks up, then down the street. 'Quinn has put in a request to have all the buildings on this strip approved for a new business. What's it called, Dale? It says in the file.'

'"The Uncanny Valley Club. Where your dreams come true." Sounds like a brothel?' She looks to Henry.

He presses his lips together as if he's not sure.

She turns to Vince. 'You?'

In the rear-vision mirror, Henry sees Vince nod his head.

'Damn right it does,' Vince says, because it does, of course, sound like a brothel.

Henry knew it wouldn't be long before Quinn got involved in a business to support his sex-doll production. It makes sense, although Quinn had feigned non-involvement when he requested Henry manage the planning application. He explained it's a company QRC is assisting. Henry let Quinn believe he's that stupid, but he's unsure why Quinn would need to keep it on the quiet.

'Not. Our. Problem,' Henry says quietly, as much to himself as to Dale.

≈

Dale follows Henry into the building, leaving Vince in the car to wallow in his disappointed that there's no pub. In the main bar she steps on shards of broken glass in her high shoes, grinding it further into the threadbare carpet. The air is nasty with the stench of old beer. Sunlight streams in the front windows catching in the broken glass and sending flashes of light throughout the building. The sprinkling sound of a guitar ditty comes to them from the back of the building, and a mix of voices—loud and soft, male and female—that becomes louder as the owners of those voices answer one another, coming closer to Dale and Henry.

As they return to the car, Vince is hanging his elbow out the window, with one of Henry's vintage cigarettes clamped between his fingers. 'I'm no expert,' he says to them, 'but that was a quick inspection.'

'Should you report them?' Dale asks. She waves a hand at the 'them', who can now be seen with faces pressed, noses squashed, glaring from the smudged front windows of the building.

Henry laughs. The squatters are dressed in what they think of as unique punk, with fanned mohawks and oversized safety pins, but compared to the original punks, they're freshly washed, cashed up and go home in the early evening to eat a wholesome dinner.

There was a time when Henry would have dealt with it, just because he could, but his interest in showing up for anything unnecessary to the job is waning. He used to be first in, his fingerprints on everything that needed doing. He wonders now if his industrious self was getting the work done, or calling attention to his abilities in search of Quinn's praise? Quinn has a way of making people want to please him. He carries an aura of judgement about him.

Vince offers his cigarette to Dale, who takes it as though this is routine for them. She climbs between the seats to get into the back to sit with him, presumably so they can share Henry's cigarettes. His rare cigarettes. The interaction is faintly disturbing.

'No need to look too deep into the building,' Henry answers. 'It's a formality job, so Quinn can tick it off. I've viewed the property. It's perfect for the purpose. We'll meet with council for them—job done. I get the sense it's one of those jobs Quinn is more connected to than he's willing to say. There's a lack of information and a distinct hurry-up attached. I'm technically in charge of this planning application, but in reality, I'm not. I'm a tool in whatever sordid deal Quinn and Benny are drumming up.'

Henry drives off and weaves his car back through the streets.

Dale either wants to display eagerness or she is eager. 'Who's the planning minister?' she asks from the back seat.

'Clarisse Eastman. Quinn wants it done yesterday,' Henry says.

'Is it a hard ask?'

'Shouldn't be.'

To be honest (a state he keeps to himself), it's been harder lately than it should be. This is partly a lack of integrity from the start-up businesses that he's required to work with—for some reason, start-ups that purchase bots get cagey about other elements of their business. There's no good reason for it, but bot businesses have a habit of neglecting things, as though they're so excited about the bots, they can't concentrate on accounting. But it's also partly his own lacklustre efforts.

He presses the accelerator and closes in on the back of a canary-yellow self-drive. Vince's lips smatter erratically to the words of a song, and Dale puts her feet up on the back seat. The right words to tell her to take her feet off his antique upholstery don't reveal themselves to Henry. He's close to giving her feet a shove with the back of his hand. People treat his car like trash. He presses the accelerator, and then pulls back to let his front bumper-band come up against the back of the self-drive, just to give it a little rub.

'What are you doing?' Dale asks evenly.

Vince reaches forward and takes the back of the seat in his hands to steady himself. 'Best you hold on,' he says to her.

Dale moves her feet to the floor and presses a hand to the back of the seat, catching Henry's eye in the mirror. With her free hand, she points to her now purple forehead.

He holds his hands casually on the steering wheel, loosey-goosey; his fingers curl tightly around it; he darts his car out to pass the self-drive; and then he dips his left arm. His car shoots to the left, in a short jab, which is enough to punch the corner of the self-drive with his bumper-band. The self-drive kicks off into a spiral and is flung across the road and into the curb.

Henry smiles at the show he's created in the rear-vision mirror. The self-drive bounces off the curb, then for added entertainment, flips and lands with the sound of snapping plastic as it skids along the gutter, upside down, and comes to a halt—once full of life, but now dead.

Vince smacks the back of the seat in delight, saying, 'That's it!' as they turn back to retrieve the data trap.

9

—

Henry & Dale

Henry and Dale sit side by side on the hallway bench, like a pair of barn owls. Henry has always liked the orange-and-green undercoat on these walls. The paintwork's completion date has been the subject of betting odds in the community for years. Henry has heard it used as a light-hearted opening to the tricky political negotiations that go on in this building: *So, those walls done yet?'* Nobody owns up to favouring the walls never being completed for the win, but there've been a few. Henry hands Dale a coffee, the warm one.

'What's your plan, Dale?' He points his coffee at Councillor Eastman's door across the chamber's hallway. The sign has been slid to 'Available', which Henry knows doesn't mean she's actually available, but rather signals 'I'm in here!' Much like a toilet, you can't go in unless you're invited.

Dale relaxes against the wall behind her seat. 'I'll put Clarisse at ease. I'll take the power out of the play.'

'Power *is* the play,' he responds. 'You need to take control of the conversation. Be confident in the product. You've read the details. You're across it all. It's an excellent product, correct?'

Dale rolls her eyes. 'I'll take control by putting her at ease.'

'We're going around in circles.'

She shrugs, and sips her coffee.

Henry's eyes meander up the wall opposite them. The plaster sags near the ceiling, with water damage from rain seeping in at the corners after every heavy downpour; Henry never stands near it. One day it'll fall in at the slam of a door.

Dale will stuff this meeting right up. How can she not? She's an intern, and Clarisse is a professional. Dale is a student, armed with nothing but theory, and Clarisse hates social bots. Quinn would be ropable if he knew Henry had given in to Dale taking the lead.

Henry licks a finger and rubs the coffee stain on his pants. 'This isn't a rehearsal; this is business. We're in the real world. We're not at school here.'

'Don't you even think about taking back my moment now, Henry.'

Is she laughing? She looks like she's laughing. Henry's plans of a win today have disintegrated. He should have changed his pants this morning; it's a bad omen.

'Don't worry. If I mess this up, I'll leave Quinn Corp. immediately.'

'If Quinn gets wind of this, it'll be me leaving immediately.'

'I'll get it done.' She thrusts her coffee at him and bangs the paper cup against his in a pact. 'You don't even have to come into the meeting. This is how confident I am.' She crosses her legs, baring a tattoo on the inside of her ankle. It's a common one; he's seen it on Esther, and many women in this town have the same one.

'Is that *Vitruvian Woman*?'

She ignores him, glances at her ankle and laughs. 'Trust me, I *will* close this deal for you.'

Henry laughs too. He tries to dig deep and muster concern, but he can't seem to raise enough to care as much as he should.

'Thanks,' she says, 'for the coffee.' The kaleidoscope egg on her forehead moves as she speaks. She leans toward him. 'I've done this kind of thing before. This internship with QC is an annoying formality, a prerequisite for a job that I already own. You can relax, Henry. Really, trust me. I'll get this done for you.'

It occurs to Henry that she won't care a jot if she fails here today: it means nothing to her. And he has nobody to blame. Vince meant well with his 'Go on, Henry; let her do the work if she wants to.' This could end with a job loss for him, which lifts his spirits, but at the same time, it would be inconvenient.

Clarisse's door opens. Dale flinches, and Henry touches her sleeve to keep her in the seat. Clarisse's steps pop on the buckling linoleum as she passes by them, and Benny, the sex-doll-salesmen slash therapist, scurries rattily out of her office behind her.

Benny doesn't appear to see Henry, which suits Henry fine. Benny shakes Clarisse's hand. 'Thank you. This is really great; thank you,' he says, and he gives a little bow of capitulation.

Henry has seen this from Benny before. It's his best fake-humble.

His floppy hair shudders about like that of an Afghan hound as he shakes Clarisse's hand and then spins around to leave, bouncing on the balls of his toes as he heads out of the building and down the front steps, his head gradually lowering until he's gone. Clarisse retreats into her office with a glance of acknowledgement directed their way.

Henry leans back. He's used to being left to sit on the bench seat, waiting for Clarisse to give him the time of day.

≈

The door opens again, and Dale is on her feet with her hand outstretched. Her coffee flicks a tiny spray across the floor onto Clarisse's boots. 'Dale,' she announces herself to Clarisse.

This awkward moment of flying coffee gives Henry the impulse to move. 'Clarisse, this is my new intern.' He speaks from behind her like a concerned parent.

Dale, bless her, doesn't falter at this interjection.

'Oh goody, fun.' Clarisse opts for her default mode of sarcasm. She waves them into her office.

'What was that about?' Henry asks Clarisse, and he nods in the direction Benny has gone.

'You don't know?' Clarisse laughs. 'You should look into that, Henry.' She sits behind the desk and moves the conversation seamlessly to the matter of The Uncanny Valley Club. 'You know, Dale, there's a large vocal—and influential, I might add—group in this town who are pro-cyborg and anti-robot.' Clarisse waves at them to sit down. 'And it's those people who have put me in this seat. I'm expected to uphold the views of the cyborg movement and dampen robot projects wherever I can.'

Henry can't let that one slide. He leans in to speak. 'It simplifies conversations to see it that way, but it's not an "us and them" argument, Clarisse. Robots and cyborgs have more in common than you think. Prime example: the mastoid mechanism, which is a cyborg development and controlled by the dots installed behind the human ear, is also the current method used for a brain in robots. This town loves to pit the two areas against each other, but in the details, they're not exclusive.'

'Thanks for the insight, Henry.' Clarisse turns to Dale. 'What you're asking me to do is approve a nightclub. A nightclub that sells time with sex dolls. It's not what you call a family tourist attraction, is it?' Clarisse smirks.

Dale laughs, though at what, Henry isn't quite clear about.

He drags his chair in closer to the desk as a reminder to them both that it's actually him that Clarisse will ultimately be talking to about this.

'So, that's my position, Dale. Go ahead and do your job: persuade me, sell it to me. Go on,' urges Clarisse.

This isn't the usual Clarisse format. Henry has attended dozens of meetings with her over the years, and this time, Clarisse has waived her usual aggressive, facts-on-the-table negotiation and honest, back-and-forth discussion, in favour of what? Listening?

Dale appears to be rattled and lost for words, and then she draws breath and takes in Clarisse's invitation to sell the sex-doll industry to her. What an ask.

'This is precisely why the town needs a business like this. I'm with you, Clarisse. On the face of it, sex-doll businesses are not the way forward for a town that values a family-friendly culture, but you know what? People just love the bots. Everybody is fascinated by a robot. Don't get me wrong, the very same people will say, "How do I know if I can trust it?" or, "I want things to be real. This is not biology," while they thump their hearts with a clenched fist and quote nationalism. But there's no way we can thwart the pull of fascination; we just can't.'

Clarisse is all ears. Henry nods at nothing in particular, and Dale nods too, as though they've agreed. Henry breathes out because, well, this is so easy.

Dale leans forward in her chair. 'And these robot nightclubs like The Uncanny Valley Club keep the sex dolls out of our homes, and listen, this is where we do have the power. This is what I know for sure: the clubs don't want the sex dolls in homes either. They want the punters in their clubs, not at home fiddling with a robot.'

Henry glances at Clarisse—nothing.

'Allowing a club like this to function will curb the take-up of bots in homes and put them where the community can control them, away from family environments.' Dale waits.

Clarisse leans back in her chair and folds her arms.

'Clarisse, I don't like it any more than you do,' Dale says. 'But if we don't put these clubs out in the open, they'll go underground. They're legal, and they're a part of a city's life. Let's take control and keep them on record. You shouldn't have an issue with the location, as the property is way down in the industrial triangle.' Dale stops talking.

Silence.

Dale glances from Henry to Clarisse and back, as if waiting for applause.

Henry gives it to her: clap, clap, clap, clap, clap. Both sets of eyes glance at him.

Clarisse smiles. Friendliness has never before leaked into this office while he's been present. Not. Ever.

'Unless there's opposition from the community,' Clarisse states, 'I can't see you coming up against any blocks for this to go ahead. If I were you, I'd get your client's paperwork done before protest groups have a chance to get in front of this. Make it happen.' Clarisse nods at Dale.

'Okay.' Dale shifts in her seat and places her hands on the arm rests, ready to leave.

'Make it happen?' Henry asks.

'You should be pleased, Henry. You don't want me to go hard on the intern, do you?' queries Clarisse.

Dale stands up along with Clarisse, and they shake hands as though it's already a done deal.

Clarisse ushers them out the door. Her acceptance of The Uncanny Valley Club is too easy; it shouldn't have been so smooth.

It lacks the negotiation, compromise and fast talking from everybody concerned, as well as the time to give the community a chance to voice their views about a business as controversial as this. But Henry says nothing. The meeting has gone their way—Quinn will be pleased.

Dale's mood is buoyant as they leave the building. She gives Henry a sideways I-told-you-so look and raises one hand. Henry is afraid she's actually going to high-five him. She touches one finger to the lump on her forehead.

They don't speak further on it, but this was the quickest turn-around and the shortest meeting in all his dealings with council. If there's been a pre-meeting discussion between Clarisse and, well, anybody, he doesn't want to know about it.

It's ridiculous to think it, but the idea that this entire meeting has followed a script creeps into Henry's thoughts. It was so smooth and clean. Dale requested, albeit playfully, the chance to lead, no question, but when it comes down to it, this happened because he didn't care enough about it. He was relieved she wanted to. This result is accidental. They caught Clarisse on a good day.

≈

Once back in the car, Henry sends a message to Quinn: 'Benny met with Clarisse before me. Know what that's about?' He doesn't get an answer, nor does he expect one.

10

Henry & Benny

Henry's phone rings on a continuous loop. Early in his tenancy at QRC, he never took Benny's call. He couldn't see how it was necessary. At most, he thought it an option. But a summons to Quinn's office by way of a scheduled meeting that had mysteriously appeared in his diary changed all that.

When he'd arrived in Quinn's doorway. Quinn motioned him to come stand by his desk. He wasn't invited to sit. Quinn silently pulled up the Fat Contract—known around the office as 'The FC'—an odd book kept in paper format that's full of expectations of loyalty, behavioural requirements and colleague pacts, which staff are expected to know—and follow—no questions asked, and which Henry dreams of putting in front of a union rep one day.

Quinn held his finger under a sentence. Henry leaned in to read: 'Employees must engage with the QRC counsellor, weekly, for the health of the staff and the health of the company.' That was all that was done. No words from Quinn. That was the first and only time Quinn admonished him for not taking Benny's calls.

His phone stops buzzing. He'd like to put Benny off for a few weeks, but it's time to allow a call, or two or three, to get through. The phone quivers again, and he puts it to his ear. 'Yup.'

'Henry! It's Benny!'

'I know it's you, Benny.'

'Why don't you say, "Hello Benny," if you know it's me?'

'Why don't I say, "Hello Benny"? Because we know who we are.' Henry holds the phone at arm's length and stares at it.

'Henry?' Benny's voice squeaks through the phone.

Henry puts it back to his ear.

'Henry? Are you there? What's that noise?'

'It's a bad line, Benn. Shall I call you later?'

'It's good now, clear as a bell. So, how are you? You sound muffled; are you in the bog?'

'No, I am not in the toilet, I'm—'

'In bed? Are you in bed? This is why we need to talk, Henry. I have an idea that you'll love—'

'No. Jesus, Benny, I'm sleeping. Can't I sleep?'

'Sleeping? What's wrong with you, Henry?'

Henry is unsure of how a therapist should behave, but he's certain Benny has no clue how a therapist should behave either. This isn't unfounded paranoia. There are signs, apart from the fact that the therapy sessions are never in person. There's the nature of the sessions, which range from two-minute check-ins to hour-long chats about robot races, vintage cars and Benny's obsession with social bots. Most alarming is the fact that, whenever Henry speaks with Quinn, Quinn is familiar with more details about Henry's life than he could or should be which obviously comes to him via Benny. Beyond that, Benny simply lacks the tact expected of a therapist. Henry pushes his pillows up to create a back rest and leans into them. But Benny is right, sleeping in the middle of the day is probably not a productive way to live, especially three days in a row, but Benny doesn't need to know that.

'Henry?'

'Yes, I'm here.'

'What's wrong with you? I mean, I know what's wrong with you, and while we're on that topic—'

'We aren't on that topic.'

'—with my new venture, your problem will be a thing of the past, and yes, I did say "will", not "could", but it *will* be in the past.' Benny coughs.

'Do you need to cough every time you mention it? It's not an undercover mission. Here's the thing, Benny: I don't need to bore you with my shit, and I'm over it. I wish I'd never mentioned it to you. My problem is no longer your problem, which means it's no longer up for discussion.'

'Henry, please talk to me. Quinn expects me to listen to your boring shit, and it sounds to me like you're screaming for help, inside, deep down—you know, in the corners of your—'

'Benny, you will note in your little diary that we spoke today, yes? And we'll put this session behind us.'

'Whatever it is that ails you today, I'm certain I can guess what lies beneath it. It's this Little Problem that you sweep under the rug. You've tucked yourself up in bed. I bet you're even in the foetal position. This tells me that this decision you've made to ignore your problems means you've shut the door on your recovery.'

'Recovery? That's an extreme word for what we do.'

'We've only just begun, Henry. I'd like to tell you that I've got an exciting new pathway, which is just right for you. I mean, Henry, you have no idea how tailored to you this is. But I can't introduce you to it yet; it's still in the pipes, and just know that this will change everything for you, okay? Don't give up on us yet.'

'Benny, this is what I love about you. You sound like you're saying something useful, but you aren't, and if I'm not careful, I'll miss this fact and waste my time trying to understand exactly what it is you're trying to say.'

'Anyway, Henry, your time's up.'

'Well, this is new. Since when do we have time limits?'

'Since I waste my time calling you multiple times with no answer. You need help, and I can move things along for you, but in the meantime, there's one thing I've suggested that you haven't tried yet, have you? And I won't let you stall on this any longer.'

'If I'm understanding you correctly, Benn, my time is up.'

'I'm sure it'll not only help,' Benny continues, 'but it'll get you used to the idea that we can heal you. Look at yourself. Your problem affects your work, you're slipping, and everyone around you knows it. We can fix it. I can fix it for you. You could lose your job over this; have you thought about that?'

This is the kind of comment that validates Henry's mistrust of Benny and Quinn. There's only one person who has access to Henry's work details, and it's not Benny.

'Did you write it down when we last spoke, Henry?'

'Yes, yes; don't tell me again. I wrote it down.'

'Make sure you get the Domin. And before I go, Henry, I know you're not fond of this idea, but don't think of Domin as a fetish or a toy or a doll. She's a real solution. Don't reject the idea, stay with it, trust it and let it dwell in that head of yours. And I'll tell you something else for free: I've got a surprise for you in the very near future. This is a life-changer, and this Domin option is a process, not a fast fix. All you need to do is let me lead the way for you. Trust the process; be open to my solution.'

'You sound like a network marketer. And you know what? Your real solution is a fake human.'

'Let the idea percolate, Henry. Look her up, look her over, and look at her long and hard. We'll talk about it again soon. And answer your phone next time. Ta ta.'

'Benny, one more thing. I saw you.'

'Saw me?'

'You met with Clarisse last week. What's that you're working on?'

'Now, this is what I mean. I have things in motion; I have a plan.'

'Yes, Benny, you have things and you have plans, but what? Has Quinn offered you management of Project City?'

There's silence from Benny, and then muffled sounds as though he has his hand over the phone.

'Benny?'

And then he's back. 'Henry, this is between you and me, right? It won't go further than here, right?'

'Right.'

'Right. Quinn said that he'll give me management of Project City if you won't follow my advice. I'll call again soon, and we'll get this fix rolling, but right now, this minute, you'll go on to my site and you'll get yourself a little Domin. Right?'

'Right.'

For the first time in years, Benny hangs up first.

Henry leans forward in his bed and crosses his legs. The thought that Quinn may have given Benny, of all people, the job he was lined up for—the job that could get him out from under Quinn— had never occurred to him. He lies back down, blocks the light out with a pillow over his face and drifts back into a sleep that keeps him out cold until dusk.

11

Henry

The decision was made to turn the lights on rather than go home. A slow afternoon of drinking leaked into a boozy evening. Kids played hide-and-seek in the dark and shouted taunts at each other—'piss weak fuck-head turd'—filled with bravery under the cover of darkness. They checked in sporadically with their parents in the footy rooms, then burst out the door with guttural war cries. Occasionally, a parent would say, 'I think that one was mine.'

They drank their way through the calling of the raffle tickets and the watching of grand-final reruns on the club's new big screen, to forget the end-of-season loss. The older kids set up a bonfire—an excuse to stay outside, or they paired off into the night—the sky so sepia and out of this world.

Henry let Asia lead him by his hand into the black. Shoes squelched in the damp grass. A dull glow streamed out from the football rooms, across the oval and hit the white trunks of the gums beyond the fence line. The stench of muddy grass rose about them as they walked into the centre of the oval. Between them, a bottle of beer they'd taken from under the trestle table swung to and fro in his sweaty fingers. The whites of her eyes were two bright, little moons.

Henry chewed on his fingernails. The funk of wet football leather hung around his face. They sat on the grass. Her forehead pressed against his, and her palm slid around his neck and pulled him to the ground. This girl knew what she was doing. His confidence withered.

Conscious of his weight upon her, he knew this was the moment; this was it.

But she pushed at him, shoved at his weight and squirmed out from beneath him. It was over?

He became aware of a spotlight lighting them up like a night game. The oval had become a daffodil-yellow field of light, and over the loudspeaker came his father's voice, 'Henry? *Henry?* Is that you on the oval?'

She got up, ran, jumped the fence with a netballer's leap and was gone.

His jeans in a thick tangle at his calves, his knee bones pressed together, his face in the peppery blades of grass and his butt-cheeks cooling in the night air, Henry froze as 1,000 billion parental faces with white teeth, stretched pink lips and shining eyes circled the boundary line to look at him.

≈

Light from the kitchen cantered into the opening door of Henry's bedroom; touched Augustine's face, which shone with a beery glow as he stood there looking into the room; and struck Henry's cheeks. He sat up in his bed.

Augustine whispered from the door, 'Are you awake? Can we smooth things over?'

Henry wanted to say that he didn't need a smoothing over. He'd prefer to stay lumpy.

'Sorry, mate.' Augustine sat on the edge of the bed.

He'd never called him 'mate' before. Henry scrambled out of the bed and stood.

'Sit down,' his dad said. 'Take it easy.'

Henry sat.

'I'm glad you're awake.' Augustine smiled. 'My son's all grown up.' A tear drop plummeted from the end of Augustine's nose onto the bed. 'I couldn't help but notice your technique. It was a bit, shall we say'—(Henry had kicked four goals that day, so whatever his technique was, it was actually pretty good) Augustine plucked fluff from the thin blankets with fat fingers—'in need of coaching?'

'Coaching?'

'You were intent on squashing the poor girl.' He nodded and leaned in to peer into Henry's face. The bed creaked.

The light in the room darkened as his mother put her head around the door, then lightened again as she left. Seconds ticked by. The outline of his father's face was hard and believable.

'Yeah,' his father said, 'football is a great analogy,' and he took a slug of his beer, the gulp visible in his neck as he looked to the ceiling in thought.

He passed the bottle to Henry. Henry took it and rest the bottle on his thigh. Until that moment, he'd not had legal, or parental, permission to drink.

'Yeah, football… think defence. Don't let her get you before you get her. Communicate with the players—that's you and her.' He pointed at Henry, one finger firmly at Henry's eyes. 'Check if she's ready for you, mate; if not, make it easy for her to get into place, positioning—you know, that sort of thing. Keep fit; keep up your fluids.' He dragged the beer back from Henry's hand.

'Sleep on it, Henry,' he said. 'It'll all come together for you one day.' He gave Henry a push on his shoulder, rough and loving, and then he left, closing the door gently behind him as though Henry were a sleeping baby.

12

Henry & Esther

Henry hasn't chosen his songs, but neither has Esther. They huddle together like naughty children and peruse the song list. She runs her finger down the titles. It's the usual tunes: 'Radio Gaga', 'It's Raining Men' and 'Waterloo'.

Across the table, Quinn leans back in his seat, with a glass of house red watered down with a softie in one hand and the menu in the other. Quinn doesn't give a shit about what's on the song list or who sings when. He's the judge of this yearly song massacre. That's the part Quinn plays. He doesn't sing—he observes. And then he'll go home and leave the rest of them 'to have the fun' without him. He keeps himself superior. He drops the menu to the table and lays his arm across an empty seat beside him.

'I fucking hate karaoke,' Henry announces, though not loud enough to reach Quinn's ears.

'You always say that.' She slides a finger to the bottom of the song list and asks, 'The usual?'

He nods. She writes it down: 'You're the One That I Want'. They switch roles. This is how they do it. He sings Olivia's part, and Esther is John. They're fifth in line to sing.

'I'd say it's about an hour before it's our turn,' she says.

Next to Esther, Griff flips the plastic edge of the drinks menu as though he hasn't made his choice yet. Henry snatches it from him. Griff glares. Griff doesn't drink, not since what his wife calls 'the last straw'. He went missing for two days, though he was actually asleep under his self-drive in his own front yard. The abstinence is too late for Griff. He's got a permanent yellow tinge, like an aura, that Esther swears glows when alcohol is close by.

Henry reads out the names of cocktails he thinks Esther should have. 'Reasons, then you can have a Painkiller, followed by a—'

'Is there a theme here?' she asks.

'And follow with a Flying Mule.'

'What's in that?'

'Vodka, lemon juice, rice wine, ginger beer, lime and cayenne pepper.'

'Sounds healthy. That's the one I'll have; just that one.'

'Just one?'

'That one, over and over,' she confirms.

≈

The barman waits patiently, as though he's interested. Finally, Henry says, 'Four shots of Henny and gimme two Flying Mules.'

The barman drops to the floor behind the bar like a collapsing puppet. Henry fixes his eyes on the still life of colourful bottles that line the walls. The barman emerges with glasses in hand. His lips murmur as he puts Esther's drinks together.

'Give me a couple of inches of that vodka,' Henry requests, 'no ice. And shove a nice fat, juicy chunk of lime in it too.' He downs the vodka and follows it with two Hennies. One, two, like throwing back peanuts. A chill has developed in his chest over the last few weeks. He presses his palm to it. It grows bigger with each drink, not smaller. He should get a doctor to see to it.

Across the room, the glass in the entrance door glints, and Dale pushes her way in, with her full weight on the swing door. She's dressed like she's about to hit the pony trail. She's late, but she'd said she wouldn't attend at all. Henry watches from the bar as Quinn introduces her to everybody around the table. She dashes a finger at Henry in hello. The sudden intake of two shots and a vodka has him feeling like she's stroking the fog that has appeared over his eyes. He gives her an awkward military salute—it's the only response to a finger dash he can think of.

'I'll need a tray,' he says to the barman.

He takes the Hennies, two Flying Mules and another vodka back to the table.

'Get lost?' Esther enquires.

'What?'

'Did you get lost?' Esther pulls her two Flying Mules to her, tips back her neck and slides one down. She hates these work things as much as he does. This is the way they get through karaoke night—a fast drowning. Without fail, they drink until they can't drink any more, or until an awkward incident occurs and they have no option but to leave.

The song chart comes to Henry's fingers from the middle of the table. Vodka, mark two, tastes like antibiotics and cools his lips. There's nothing but ice in his glass now. It clunks on his teeth. He looks at Esther, but she's gone, on her way to the bar. He watches Esther walk, one foot carefully in front of the other like a horse. She's the best friend in the whole world to him. He'd tell her he loves her, but that's not the right words to describe it. Griff is singing 'Don't Go Breakin' My Heart' on the stage. His cheeks gleam like crotch-shined apples—he's actually crying.

Henry can't think why it is that he and Esther only ever sing one song. He's got an okay voice and he doesn't hate karaoke that much. In fact, he fucking loves karaoke. He puts his fingers to the laminated song list and flicks at a sticky noodle that was clinging to it. It lands on the stumpy soy-sauce bottle in the centre of the table. He writes 'I Go to Rio' between the number 11 spot and the number 12 on the list of singers, and then writes his name beside it. He squeezes it in using teeny, tiny writing, so small that if anybody says it's not his turn, he'll be saying, 'There, there; right there, it is,' squishing it with his fat finger until they concede.

Esther returns and passes him a drink. He takes a long slurp as though he's just come in from the desert. He can't taste what it is.

'You're walking funny, like a horse, but I still love you,' he says.

'I know; I'm wearing high heels. It's a new thing for me. I've never worn them, ever. I've been on flat heels my whole life—an anti-heelist—and now, suddenly, I want high heels, and the best ones too, expensive, and the clothes to match. Don't ask me why; I don't understand it either. I wear them in bed so that I hit the floor heeling in the morning. I know you love me. You always love me on karaoke night, about midway through the night. You're early tonight.'

'Ready?'

'After we eat. I'm not in a Travolta mood until I've had my yum cha.' Esther lurches her head looking for the waitress. 'Hey, doll!' Esther calls out.

The waitress pays her no attention.

'I'm not sure she's a doll, Esther,' Henry observes.

'Yep, she is, and so's the barman,' and then, much louder and very unlike Esther, she calls, 'Hey, dolly doll!' and then stuffs two fingertips between her lips and whistles loudly.

Henry, not quite drunk enough to be blind to the sudden attention Esther has brought them, brings his voice to a whisper, 'She looks human to me.'

'It's her eyes,' Esther explains. 'She's a Bertha model, exactly like mine.'

'Yours?'

'My doll.'

They press their heads together, temple to temple. The waitress moves in and out and around tables, with plates and glasses balanced all the way up her arm, stuck fast as though on suction cups.

'Wait for the blink. Don't you blink, Henry, or you'll miss it.'

They wait. For a very long time. Henry blinks regularly. He can't stop it now.

'See? There. Such a perfect blink,' Esther declares.

'Creepy,' he says, but he missed it because he's stuck on the idea that Esther owns a doll. She's never mentioned it to Henry, and the Bertha is no ordinary doll.

'Isn't it? Like it's a trick; like she's pulled one over us. She has the best shoes, though, and the sweetest skin. You'd think they'd give them wrinkly skin and bloodshot eyes, from working late nights in all this sickening vapour everyone sucks on lately.'

Henry and Esther perform their piece, so smooth. They've done it so many times Henry doesn't even need to think about it. Each with a hand to the other's shoulder, they push each other back, then forward, then back. It's the only move they do, and the words fall from their mouths without the need to look at the screen. Esther is a fucking great Travolta. She holds her head just right. Stiff. Smug. For three minutes, they're Danny and Sandy, or as they say to each other, Sanny and Dandy.

Henry slugs another drink down. He pulls out his phone and searches for the lyrics to 'I Go to Rio'. He looks for the words that he gets wrong. He's sure it's 'I'm a saucy fella'. He takes to the stage, untucks his shirt, unbuttons it and ties it in a tidy knot at the front. Esther laughs and claps. She's bent forward from the waist (she can't stand up straight in her high-heel shoes). It's a pretty good show, he feels. His talent has gone untapped. He could have been an entertainer. Mid-song now, he takes off his shirt and flings it across the room, his head held high like a bullfighter. Flair.

Dale glances at him. Her face is white, like a geisha.

He loved to sing when he was a child, but …

The bartender retrieves Henry's shirt in a scuffling kind of way, crablike, and places it on the floor in front of Henry while he shimmies across the stage with two forks for maracas. He's dancing, singing and thinking. He's thinking of buying maracas. So many thoughts, so many dance moves.

≈

The yum cha is almost gone. He only stopped at the bar for a moment. He only sang a few songs. He picks at what's left of a broken dim sim, sucks at a dumpling and finishes with a nice little bit of tapioca pud. It's an awkward act of nibbling titbits, under the full glare of Dale. He knew the awkward would turn up, eventually, and here it is. He's always surprised at how it arrives and who it arrives with. He returns her gaze. He can't read her. She looks as if she can read him, though. She speaks, but he can't hear what she's saying. He glances around. Esther's feet stick out from under the table, shoeless. Dale's chair is empty. She's halfway out the door.

≈

Henry peers at his door-locks. He takes a considered moment to get his fingers to insert the key and turn it. The door opens. The couch is close. He lays himself out flat and yells, '*Screen on!* A black-and-white movie. Atticus speaks to Scout. Like a father should, just like it. A sob escapes Henry's throat, and the couch grows wet around his face. He imagines himself as a father teaching a child to ride a bike; the image is his favourite cliché.

≈

The Domin model is tiny on his screen, but real—like a real woman. Benny told him if he tried her out, he'd figure out exactly how his erectile dysfunction does its devious work against him, with no attachments and no emotions, just the flick of eyelids and the loyalty of a dog. Skin on skin. Raw.

He's heard that Quinn keeps a bunch of them in his home for parties. Esther only dared to whisper it to him, hot puffy air in his ear. Parties so out there that Esther didn't want to recall all the sordid details to him, just a few dark titbits. Esther gets called in to manage the trauma clean-up (she's the one Quinn trusts). She has a team—Olly Bizwell is on her team. Henry doesn't know why Olly Bizwell is needed for a party clean-up. He doesn't want to know, but Esther did mention that Olly is needed for both his cunning and his strength.

He saw Bizwell in the flesh once. He breezed into QRC, all nonchalant, minutes after they'd coincidently—or not—had their day interrupted by a story breaking on the news feed: *Olly Bizwell's Criminal Law Leaks.*

Olly walked in and was like, 'Hey Esther,' as he swished on past into Quinn's office. He needed no direction.

'What the fuck, Esther?' Henry had demanded.

'Olly's on my team,' she had said calmly, as though it was a conversation about wine preference.

Henry had replied with, 'What the fuck?' again.

But that was all Esther would say.

They had cause to watch news on Olly again two months later when he was acquitted. Esther's mouth had fallen open. Everybody in the office had looked at her as though her response would explain his getaway, but all she had said was, 'Wow.'

Henry has heard Quinn say, 'You're only remembered for creating humankind or destroying humankind.' He wonders, which is it that Quinn and Olly do together—creating or destroying? Does he destroy humankind with the creation of robots, or does he create a better human? He thinks of Benny in that meeting with Clarisse. He's pretty sure those two together were all about destruction.

He touches one finger to the purchase tab. A red number 1 appears in the shopping cart. Earlier, he and Esther had pushed each other back and forth across the stage, hands to shoulders, singing. Dale watched them both, and she watched Esther's treatment of the doll, after which Dale remained seated, rigid and cool as a cucumber. She spooned honeyed prawns between her teeth, avoiding the stickiness by keeping her lips in a permanent 'O'. Henry felt her gaze for the rest of the night. Everybody has an opinion on the dolls, but he's not sure what Dale's true opinion is.

How close he's come to buying Domin frightens him. He throws his phone across the room. It hits the wall and thuds to the floor. Little, blue pieces of broken phone shoot across the room, making soft, tinkle noises as they land.

13

Benny, Penny, The Butler & Quinn

'Penny, will you take a hit?' Benny queries her.

Between her thumb and finger, Penny holds a toothpick, weighted down by an army-green olive with a delightful little pop of dark-red capsicum inside. She stirs her martini slowly. Okay,' Benny ponders, 'it's a bit of a cliché, the olive and the martini, but punters love clichés when it comes to bots. Their minds connect it with humanness, so they feel good about the situation: the whole 'having sex with plastic' situation.

'A hit?' she queries him.

Benny flicks his screen up.

Penny pokes the olive into her mouth and her smooth lips close around it, then she whisks the toothpick out, flamboyantly holds it up high between them and lets it drop to the table. It could be a fault in her system that has her do this, but Benny is on to it quick smart—she's mimicking her version of a mic drop.

Benny rolls his eyes at her, but he's delighted by the Penny's antics. She grins, her luminescent teeth glow like pearls. She gulps the olive down her throat, unchewed and whole.

Benny taps the screen to open his website. 'You eat olives,' he states, without looking at her.

'I eat anything you do, Benny.'

'What about scruples? Do you have scruples?'

'Scwooples?'

'You know, do you have morals? Are you righteous?'

'I tawt you meant do I eat scwooples, Benny.' She laughs, picks up another toothpick and spears another dry olive from the bowl in the centre of the table.

'What I want to know, Penny, is are you a feminist? Will you take a hit or two?'

Penny stirs her martini anti-clockwise this time. She stops to raise her face to him. Her chin held high, she says, 'What's the qwestion, Benny? Are you asking me if I permit harm on my body?'

'That's the question; spot on. But keep in mind you're all wires and plastic—I can't actually harm you, can I? Nothing that can't be fixed, eh?'

'I have thwee answers for you, Benny.'

'Just give me the one I need to hear.'

'Being a feminist means fair, wight and eqwal, doesn't it? You walked in here today, and you told me you're a fair man. It was the third sentence you said to me. "I'm a fair man, Penny," you said to me. Were you lying? Are you a fair man?'

He's about to justify to her how he moves within his version of the world, but her eyes flicker, and he decides he doesn't need to explain himself to a doll. He looks at her neck. It's thinnish, and her chest is medium-ish. He leans to look under the table, pushing his floppy hair from his eyes to get a good look at her. From the waist down, she's thick and short, like a bowling pin. Most of her weight is below her middle, for stability. She doesn't know it, but she's built for rough handling. If she took a punch, she'd swing back to right way up, like a punch doll.

She nods at his pause. 'I know my wight from wong,' she says in her Brooklynese, baby-talk voice. 'If you bweach laws, human or andwoid, I'll block physical engagement.' She leans back in her seat and crosses her arms against her chest.

Perhaps her sense receptors take Benny's lack of response as befuddlement, and she seeks to explain. 'Let's unpack this a wittle bit for ease of your compwehension. If you harm me, Benny, and I belong to you, that's stupidity—I'm expensive. If I don't belong to you, I'm the property of somebody else, so that's illegal. And Benny, The Wobotics Convention states that, in the case of andwoid pwoducts, those made in the image of the human must be tweated as the same, and are pwotected by law, as a human.'

Benny exaggerates a double take. 'Are you kidding me, Penny? Nobody believes that shit, and that's four answers, not three.'

Penny mimics his double take. 'Four, thwee, whatever, Benny; I know our law.'

'What's the point there, Penny? I mean, "made in the image of" doesn't mean "the same as", and nobody pays mind to those laws. They're a formality; they don't mean anything.'

'With deepest wespect, Benny, you humans are not complex. In your mind, the idea of "made in the image of" does actually mean "the same as". You anthwopomowphise to understand the world awound you, and The Wobotics Convention wecognises that human twait. To make sense of a welationship with a doll, you humans subconsciously see bots as acting, feeling and behaving as though they're weal. You people know that a doll isn't weal, but your subconscious engages with it as if it is.' She laughs. 'That makes you so cwoss, doesn't it?'

Benny taps his dots and types 'anthropomorphise meaning' into his eye screen rather than his hover, so Penny can't see. He watches her face. Nah, he knows she's not real.

'And there's a weason for these laws, Benny. They're not to pwotect me; they're to pwotect you, get it? If you humans emotionally engage in an expewience with a doll, when you turn around and walk out the door, you're so base that you'll wedirect the feelings you had with a bot to a similar expewience with a human. Do you wead me, Benny? You can't help yourself.' Penny throws her head back and laughs. 'Shall I make it simple for you? If you hit me, you're likely to, in a similarly emotional ciwcumstance, also hit a human, and in the case of the scenawio you're asking me to expewience here, hit with eqwal vulgarity.'

Benny taps his dots down. 'Humans aren't that stupid. We know the difference between a human and a doll.' Benny pinches his arm. 'I'm real,' he says, and then leans across the table and raps his knuckles on her forehead. 'You're plastic.'

'Don't take offence to what I tell you, Benny. I know you awen't stupid.' Penny twitches, as though she struggles with honesty. 'But we could converse for hours about suspension of disbelief, where it begins and where, if at all, it ends, but let's keep it simple. I happen to know simple is easiest for you, Benny—listen, if I'm not weal, why're you affected by what I say?' She slips another olive in her mouth and mic-drops the toothpick.

'Well, that *does* make it simple, doesn't it? I don't think you're the girl for me then, Penny.'

Penny shows no sign of caring. It's neither here nor there for her. She takes another olive and stirs her drink and gazes around the room. Her silky hair sways. It's clean and sexy. It's a shame she won't take a hit. Benny likes her—she reminds him of himself a little bit.

The sales stats on his screen tell Benny that his business is running at a loss, which will be excellent come tax time, but for now, there's no cash to splash—which isn't so great when it comes time to pay what he owes on the building works for the club. His outdated bot stock remains on the shelf, becoming more and more out of fashion by the second, like old cheese. They're kinda what people want, but they're not popular. Everybody wants to get a look at the new Domin now.

'Penny, my Uncanny Valley Club will be a joint full of bored punters and no dolls if I can't come up with the cash.'

'I'm sowwy to hear that, Benny. What may I do to help?'

He shrugs, 'Well, if you told me you're a dirty skank instead of a righteous feminist, and for the same price, that'd help. But you didn't, did you?' His phone vibrates in his pocket for the third time since he sat down with the Penny. It's Quinn, and Quinn can wait.

Quinn's sales plans reward Benny with one free basic model doll if he sells any five dolls in a week. Two free, if he sells eight. He can sell the old cheeses off cheap and earn enough to put into a few advanced social bots for the club. He needs a few in the bar, a few in the booths and a few in the suites. He slides back to the web and releases the ads Esther wrote for him:

Best-quality sex therapy. Confidential. Private. Discreet.
Best-selling author of You, Your Schlong and AI.
BENNY_LIBERANSKI_ROBOT.COM

No time? Your robot can do it all for you. The three Cs:
Cleaning. Cooking. Company.
BENNY_LIBERANSKI_ROBOT.COM

He's had over 60,000 hits on the new Domin since he advertised her, but as yet, only two purchases. She's so real she intrigues, but she also scares. Punters like the idea of owning her, but they want to be sure she won't own them. He needs to get her on the floor of the club so people can try her out and know the control is in their hands.

Penny's shoulders shrug. The corners of her mouth turn down. He puzzles over this for a moment, then sees that it's him she's reflecting.

'You learn fast, Penny.'

'Yes, I do. It's compounding intelligence, just like you, but I'm never too tired, aged or disintewested to wetwieve.' Penny winks.

He laughs at her; the wink is cute. His phone jangles in his pocket again. 'It fucking annoys me to be available at all times, Penny.'

'You need a secwetawy, Benny; somebody like me.'

He digs his phone out of his pocket. 'Sorry, I should take this,' he says, and then smiles. He doesn't need to apologise to her, for anything.

Quinn talks before Benny has a chance to speak. 'Benny, time is upon us. I need to move on appointing an overseer for Project City. I want it to be Henry. Please tell me he's got his act together—and keep in mind, his work is showing me that he hasn't.'

Penny nods demurely at Benny. 'I'm on sale today,' she whispers. 'Only today. They're upgwading me. You won't be in a position to afford the new Penny, will you, Benny?'

Benny frowns at her. She has attitude, but he'd prefer her to be more aggressive, more dynamic. 'Sassy' is the word he's looking for. He likes her, though. She's got a nice tinge of orange to her hide. He could work her behind the bar. She'd glow under the lights. The price can't be ignored, and she could manage a job like that.

'Quinn, I think we can safely say that Henry is on his way; he's almost ready. We're waiting to put him through the club experience. But listen, I've got a great idea for Project City.'

'Now, Benny, I don't need any new ideas, especially your ideas.'

'You don't think you do, but I'm thinking the club is really going to take off. I've got interest in it through the website—bus tours, buck's parties and hen's nights—and get this idea, Quinn: The Uncanny Valley Club within the walls of Project City? I could sell you a franchise; mate's rates?'

'Project City is mapped out; there's no room in it for your club.'

'They'd come to my club in droves for the experience and stay in your Project City to take in all of what you're selling there. The club isn't just for leisure, Quinn. It's medicinal. It's therapeutic—look at what we'll do for Henry.'

'Benny, I'm aiming for taste, class and quality. Come to think of it, that could be our sub tag: TCQ. And it's already approved. I can't make changes. As awesome as your club sounds, it's not taste and class, is it?'

'Don't say no, Quinn. No one will notice if you slip an Uncanny Valley Club in here and there.'

'I won't say no, but I won't say yes either. You show me what the club can do, get it off the ground, and we'll see. Let's talk about Henry. You're telling me Henry is almost ready, but I'm telling you this: Esther says he's not up to it. She's telling me he's incapable of reading a contract, let alone actioning one.'

Penny lifts her drink to her mouth. Her lips press against the glass like a snail on a window. No drops will get through that suction. He hoped she'd take a sloppy, careless, big gulp, and then let it dribble down her chin, her neck and down her chest. She sips demurely, like his grandmamma would.

'I haven't spoken to him this week,' Benny says.

'I'm told he was a total messy bitch at our karaoke night. He kept that under wraps until I vacated the event, but apparently, he pretty much only stepped off the podium to get himself another drink. He serenaded the entire restaurant all night with every cheesy song you can think of.'

'Hold on a sec, will you?' Benny pulls the phone away.

Penny rests her chin on her hands and smiles a quarter smile—nice. She reaches out, takes the wine bottle and trickles wine into his glass. Her frozen eyes measure it. The pale fluid hits the widest part of the glass, and she stops pouring.

Quinn breathes heavily into the phone with annoyance.

'But, Quinn, Henry is in control. I'd say he was acting a part, playing the loose cannon for the fun of it. He's a fun guy, that Henry. Liked by everyone. I'd be inclined to say he's a highly intelligent observer of situations, confident and almost ready to go. I'd hazard a guess he's working on who he might take with him if he takes the reins at Project City. Which is good, right? He's perfect for the position of permanent resident and manager, and I'll have his Little Problem sorted for you lickety-split.'

Benny decides he likes Penny for the job of a cheap bargirl. She's stupid but reliable, and cute.

'I'm hearing you, Benny, and don't think I don't know what you're doing for us here. I owe you for this.'

'Yep, Quinn, he's definitely your man.'

Benny's not sure if this is true, but the benefits of having Henry as a client of the club are enormous. Besides his upcoming performance for the salty video Scottie has ordered, Henry has contacts, and once he's hooked, he'll defend and promote the place like an ice addict to his dealer.

The Butler appears beside Benny and leans in close, slightly touching Benny's cheek with his rubbery nose. The Butler lacks in the spatial-awareness area. 'Any questions about the Penny I may answer for you, sir?' The Butler is a bit basic, but he's so clean, crisp as an apple and holds mountains of data. He's adorable. Benny loves the showroom themes—it's a true adult fairyland.

'Where are you, Benny?' Quinn asks. 'Is that the Butler I can hear? Are you in the showroom?'

'Well, since you ask, I'm at your showroom to stock up on dolls for the club—on account, of course, as I'm still waiting for your money to come through. In fact, why don't you call in a bit of credit for me while I'm here? Easy-peasy.'

'Hang on. Back it up, Benny—I've already given you a loan, *and* bots rent free. The deal is that you make Henry whole, and pending those results, I'll inject further funds.'

'Quinn, mate, we just clarified that Henry is good to go.'

'Let me quote you from but five minutes ago, "He's all but sorted." Benny, when he's sorted, not *all but sorted*, you will get your money. I'm a man of my word. You know that.'

'The thing is, Quinn, I can't have Henry going in dicks ablaze without the whole atmosphere, and believe me, he's champing at the bit. He's totally eager. If you could help me out here a bit? It's almost ready. I've done the business plan; I sent it to you. It pans out, right? Good to go; ready to rumble. And the building works are done, all I need is—'

'I tell you what, Benny, you're right. You need to get Henry in top shape for me: help him get his confidence back. Do what it takes, talk him through it and stir up his drive—be the therapist you're supposed to be. But you need to drop everything else you're working on and do me a little favour, and I'll do you one. I'm send-ing Olly Bizwell to you. Give him a few freebies in your new club—something real classy, like—and tell him it's a favour from me, from Quinn, righto?'

'Olly Bizwell? What do I get in return? It'd better be an Olly Bizwell-sized favour.'

'This is what I'll do for you, Benny. Is the Butler there? Put him on for me.'

Benny holds his phone to the Butler. 'He wants to talk to you.' The Butler leans in and stares at the screen. 'No, no,' Benny directs. 'Your ear; put your ear on it. Take it; take it in your hand.'

The Butler smiles at Quinn's voice. He nods and nods, and nods again. 'Yes, Quinn. Okay, Quinn,' he says. 'Yes, Quinn, I will do. Bye-bye, Quinn.'

Benny loves watching the Butler in action. He loves watching any doll in action. He leans back in the chair, flicks hair from his eyes and puts his hands behind his head. 'I fucking love you dolls. To think I can spend my days working in your world. I fucking love yous all.'

The Butler hands the phone back. 'Quinn says to take you to the warehouse and give you a thorough look at what's available to you. Shall we go to the warehouse, Benny?'

14

Henry, Domin & Vince

Henry's finger hovers over the Bertha model, then the Karel, and finally, comes to pause over the Domin. Domin is different. The Karel are generic street bots with gangly legs, hard skin and wiry hair. Bertha is well, Bertha. Domin's hair is the rich colour of aged copper with flecks of dirty black. It's shaved at the back and angled away from her small, fierce eyes. The generics have large doll eyes that make a mockery of the transaction. Domin's skin is pale; her mouth is toothy. She has a look of loyalty, but then, Henry may have read too much into this idea of Domin; these dolls don't offer loyalty. These dolls don't feel *at all*. As he thinks this, the word 'feel' catches his attention. Henry leans in to read the caption under Domin: 'How do you want me to feel?' she asks this of anybody who takes the time to read it. Henry sits back. Want *her* to feel? Henry is certain this is a mistake; it should say 'How do you want me to make *you* feel?'

Henry has a meeting coming up with Quinn soon, to—as Quinn said—get Henry up to speed on the dolls. Henry took it to mean the new project will soon go ahead, and that he's to take over the planning and management. It hadn't occurred to him there might be a new phase of dolls to get up to speed on—dolls that know how to feel.

Henry turns away from the gaze of the dolls on his screen. His apartment window flickers with shadows as flying objects move across the sky. He blinks, switches thoughts and takes notice. He feels watched over, but that may be guilt making a move on him tonight. He counts the aircraft as they pass by, but gives up counting after twenty-three. He's never seen so many transporters in this city.

Domin's image has cut a silhouette in his mind's eye. He sees her outline on the walls, the windows, the doors and in the shadows, and he's drawn back to read her description, which he skims. He doesn't want to know too deeply the details of the soft plastics for robot sex. Words jump out at him: 'durable skin', 'sliding intelligence', 'heuristic capabilities' and 'pain sensors'. The words blur. He can't bring himself to focus on the technical side of this; understanding technique has never been Henry's thing.

He runs an eye over the physical choices. There are so many: height, fingernails (long, short, painted, natural or bitten), skin colour, age, hair colour, hair length, foot length, on and on. Henry arrives at personality choice. Personality is available in two pods, A or B, but he's overwhelmed. Once a doll arrives, there are choices to be made within that pod. He doesn't want choices. He doesn't want to be her maker. Henry would like her to simply be; to exist. For Henry, creating her is admitting to personal failure. A failed human concocting a no-fuss, predictable mate.

Beyond his front door, the lift creaks as it shoots past. His face prickles at the thought of explaining himself, of describing Domin to his friends. He sits quietly in his humiliation. But there's Esther to think of. She has her own bot, the Bertha, which makes Esther the kind of person he never imagined her to be. And this is exactly why he supposes friends will judge him, as he does Esther.

Benny's proclamation that a doll will help him doesn't mean Benny is right. When it comes to Benny, the first assumption should always be that Benny is most likely wrong.

Henry closes the browser and shuts his screen. The cuckoo jumps out and squawks. It's 7:30. He thinks of Vince, down below in the lower unit.

≈

There is a new scent, not unpleasant, and it's all through Vince's home. Vanilla? Cake?

Henry calls out, 'Coming in.' He moves through the house toward the bedroom. It occurs to him the vanilla is the doll. Now, all he can smell is rubber.

Vince doesn't answer. Lying face down on his bed, Vince sighs deeply as Henry enters the bedroom.

Henry takes a seat on the edge of the bed. It's not easy to be here for Vince when his support isn't welcome, but he can't watch Vince wallow in his disgusting sheets and do nothing to help him. 'Want to come on a trip with me, Vince?'

Vince murmurs into the pillow. Henry stands up and drags the curtains open, rattling them on their tracks. Dead flies are swept from the windowsill to the floor. Vince is often vague and lethargic. He takes pills for a condition that have an effect on his clarity of mind. Henry goes into the kitchen and switches the coffee machine on. He thrusts the dishes, sticky with unidentifiable food, off the bench and into the sink. They crash and scrape.

Vince calls out to him from the bedroom, 'Don't do my dishes.'

Henry smiles at the idea that Vince thinks he might stack his dishwasher for him. His phone buzzes: 'Still good for dinner? Café Bang-Bang at 8:00? x.' He'd forgotten about Dale.

'Where's this trip to?' Vince questions. 'Mexico?'

The thing about Vince is that, when he's at rock bottom, he jokes—a lot—and as a result, Henry's worry for him dissipates. The joking isn't sincere; it's a measure of lightness to move Henry's attention away from whatever it is Vince avoids talking about.

'We could go to Mexico,' Henry replies to him. 'But first, let's go see Scottie.' Henry ponders the idea of escaping everything and taking a trip away. The idea has energy, but Henry could never be that organised.

Vince is silent.

Henry leaves the coffee and goes back to him.

'No,' Vince says. 'The answer to everything is no. No, we won't go on a trip, and no, I won't be going with you to see Scottie, but it's Tuesday, right?' Vince rolls the bedclothes back. He's dressed in a green-and-blue checked shirt and tie-dyed jeans with striped suspenders. Henry does a double take at the colourful attire, and at Vince's pants, folded neatly and pinned where his legs end.

'We're doing disco outfits now?'

Vince's hair stands in frazzled spikes. His tired, red eyes glow in the centre of painted black circles. He resembles one of the creepy clowns Henry's been seeing on street corners and in parks, loitering eerily in wait; why? Nobody seems to know, but coincidently, there's been an increase in anti-authoritarian bashings on the streets.

'Yes, it's Tuesday,' Henry concurs. He'd like to ask Vince about his clown outfit—this street-clowning is something Vince would do, but if he's standing on corners just to be creepy, Henry doesn't want to know about it. 'Let me know if you need help with your pants,' he says instead.

'What's wrong with my pants?'

'I could sew them for you instead of you pining them back. They wouldn't flap about so much.'

'You can't sew.'

'No, that's true; I can't sew.'

'What's wrong with you? You don't say things like that.'

'Like what?'

'Like *sew my pants.*'

The clumsy conversation reminds Henry of Dale's text. He pulls out his phone and texts back: 'Sorry, Dale. I forgot I'd made plans with Vince tonight.'

'Can't I care about your pants?' Henry says.

'You thinking about my pants is not okay.'

'And sorry, Vince, but we can't go to Café Bang-Bang tonight.'

'Now you're really scaring me, Henry.' Vince rolls over lethargically. 'What's wrong with Café Bang-Bang? Is it the girl? Did you show her our place?'

'She's a big girl, Vince; she found it all by herself. And she's allowed to eat.'

Vince climbs off the bed. 'And you're supposed to be a big boy, Henry. We could all eat together. How's that for an idea?' He presses his fists to the floor and moves to the bathroom. 'And you think I'm the one with problems,' Vince calls back.

He comes back within minutes—the black rings around his eyes washed away, his hair combed down and rainbow suspenders gone —and then disappears into the kitchen. Henry follows behind.

Vince sits at the dining table and fires up his old laptop. He pokes repeatedly at the screen until it comes to life. Henry goes back to making coffee and watches it trickle into two cups. The fragrance lands somewhere between ripe raspberry and dark chocolate, and it lifts his mood.

'What can I say to convince you to come meet with Scottie's psychologist? Would you have a look at her website, to see the work they do? It's amazing.' He places coffee on the table in front of Vince and sits across from him.

'Just remember I'm doing this for you, Henry.'

'Doing what?'

Vince takes a swig of coffee, swishing it in his cheeks before he swallows. 'Promise me you won't be weirded out,' he says, scrolling on his laptop.

'About what?' Henry thinks of the clown footage he's seen on the news. He's definitely weirded out about that.

Vince swivels his laptop screen around.

Henry looks at the picture of the Bertha model.

'Tell me you'll at least think about her.' Vince leans across the table to peer into Henry's face. 'Come on, Henry, play along. It'll be great for you, and you know what? We can share stories.'

Henry holds his gaze. 'We won't be sharing doll stories.'

'But you'll think about it?' Vince sits back in his seat.

Henry has considered friendly blackmail to be a reasonable option to get Vince to take an appointment at Scottie's, but perhaps a swap will do it.

'Where is she, by the way?' Henry looks around the room. 'Where do you keep her?'

'She keeps the vac warm.'

'In the cupboard?'

Vince points to a cupboard in the kitchen. 'Take a look. Re-acquaint yourself with the pleasure.'

Henry can't recall which doll Vince owns. His introduction to it was a bit of a shock. He presses his hands into his pockets, moves to the cupboard and opens the door. It's dark and smells of dust and boots. He leans into the closet then runs a hand inside, looking

for a light switch. And then her two feet are there, in high heels—
red ones. She's seated on a stool. Her eyes closed. He wonders what
being locked in a dark cupboard might do to a person. He raises a
hand to touch her, to reassure her, and then recoils. He imagines
her disappointment.

'Can she hear me?' he asks.

'No mate.' Vince laughs from behind his shoulder.

'Don't do that to me, Vince.'

'Didn't mean to scare you. I've shut her down. I only get her
going to use her.'

'Use her?' Henry shuts the cupboard. 'Doesn't she need airing or
something?'

'She's not a blanket. She actually smells pretty good, though. I
think she has some kind of deodoriser or something; I don't know.
I didn't read too much about her. You know me, I'm not one for
reading instructions.'

'You could at least let her take her shoes off.'

'Aw, see, Henry? You care for the doll. That's sweet. We're *so*
going to get you one to play with. It might help you, you know,
figure yourself out.'

'Why is it everyone thinks I need to do this? You know this is
weird, right?'

'I've heard they're good for guidance on how to get it right the
first time,' Vince explains. 'People use them for that, you know;
people who need to.'

Henry puts his hand on Vince's shoulder and guides him away
from the cupboard. 'It's not my first time, Vince.'

'Might as well be.' Vince sits at the dining table. He smooths his
hand over his head where the crazy clown hair has found its way to
spiking up again, and he grins.

Henry sits down opposite him. 'Okay, so okay.'

Vince sits up and points at the screen, 'Yeah?'

'Order me one,' Henry says.

'Don't you want to have a look at a few first?' Vince flicks and scrolls. 'Here, look at this mama—she'd show you a thing or two; perfect for meek little Henry.'

'The Domin,' Henry states. 'Get me the Domin.'

Vince laughs and taps at his laptop keys. 'Domin? You've looked, Henry? Why so coy?'

Henry crosses his legs and looks away, out the window. 'Do it before I change my mind,' he says, his heart rocking in his chest.

'Delivery or pick up?' Vince asks. 'I'll get you pick up, at the post office. You don't want her lying around at your front door for everybody to see.'

Henry reaches across the table and clasps Vince's flying fingers. 'I'll do this thing for me, if you promise you'll come see Scottie for an appointment—for you.'

'I'll come, but I won't make any promises to you or Scottie.' Vince shakes Henry's hand from his and keeps typing. 'She's been in the news, Scottie and her kind. They're on the streets. They threaten everyone who's ever used one, built one or invented one. Is Quinn aware you're chumming up with her?'

'She's not the enemy; she just has her own values and ideals. She's not a bad person.'

'Yeah … but look at the way they go about it.' Vince slides his laptop around to show pictures of Scottie surrounded by protestors. 'They're anti-bot Nazis; how is that useful?'

'I'd call it pro-enhancement more than anti-bot.'

'Semantics.' Vince swivels the laptop back to him. 'Cash-pay number, please.'

Vince enters the numbers as Henry reels them off. 'You should get your dots, Henry; these transactions would be so much easier for you.'

'Have you got your dots?'

'No, but I don't work in the industry.'

'Neither do I. I work for a guy in the industry.'

Vince raps on a key. 'Done,' he says, 'It won't be long now!' Vince dances in his seat. 'Cha-cha-bots, cha-cha-bots! Hey, why not try mine while you wait for yours to arrive? Go get her out of the cupboard.'

Henry stands up. 'That's going a bit too far, Vince. Come on. We need to get out of here. Two men in a smelly room talking about sharing bots—it's not right.' He takes Vince's wheelchair from the door and pushes it to him. 'Climb in; we're going out.'

≈

In the lift, Henry holds on to the wheelchair's handles, steadying his vertigo. The top of Vince's fat head stares outward through the lift's clear windows at buildings that glow with solar glass on every visible window and roof.

Vince points down at the community parkland, filled with the green flags of Scottie's movement—a fixture of a protest whose participants have grown in number over the weeks. 'What do they expect to get out of demonstrating to people like us?' he asks.

Henry shrugs. 'She's got your attention.'

Henry wonders what Scottie would say about him having just now purchased a doll. The Domin doll wasn't only a bargaining chip to get Vince over the line to see Scottie, it'd intrigued him enough to tip him into a purchase. He can't deny the power of the fascination.

'Can I change her name?' Henry asks Vince.

'Mate, you can call her whatever you need to, and she'll answer you in any voice, you know, that you … you know, like.'

From behind, Henry watches the skin around Vince's cheek bones slip into a grin.

The lift slides open at ground level. He follows as Vince pushes himself through the foyer and out into the dusky light of the street.

15

Benny & The Butler

With his right fingers, The Butler presses a code into his left palm to enter the doorway to the warehouse. There's no signage. The door slides open, and they duck down to pass under the low doorway. They move along the corridor that angles down, and they go deeper, deeper underground and come to another door, which is grass green and human height. The Butler stops. He pivots to face Benny. The Butler's pore-less skin moves evenly around his lips as he speaks, while resting both hands on Benny's shoulders. 'You understand that this is a non-public place? We don't show our friends this place, do we, Benny?'

The Butler prototype is, as expected, deliberate and poker-faced, but this particular Butler is Quinn's personal employee, and as such, has developed a foreboding demeanour.

'No, of course, Butler. We don't show our friends this place,' confirms Benny.

The Butler opens the door, and they enter the room. A Penny appears from behind a desk. These bots don't stand up, they rise up.

She lays her eyes on The Butler, who locks the door behind him. The click echoes into the high ceiling. This is a different Penny to the showroom Penny. It appears to be identical, but this one's personality will be in response to its particular experiences. They're like twins, triplets or even quintuplets. He wonders what it is that a group of Pennys is called: *Penny farthing? Penny Royal? Pennywise?*

Behind the Penny—high on the wall, like a work of art—is a bot with half her skin cover on and half peeled back, displaying the inner workings of her entire left side. The Santicon skeleton of the left half of her reflects warm blue from the skylight above, and the skin on her right side is dewy and fresh. Her hair, chocolate brown with Medusa-style dreadlocks, quivers in a breeze pushed out by a pedestal fan, circulating the stuffy air around and around and around.

'I've seen this one before,' Benny says. 'It's from the Adult Expo in Vegas, right?'

'The Medusa has caught your attention,' The Butler observes.

They stand before her and gaze at her.

'Is this Quinn's?' Benny asks in a high-pitched voice.

'That she is.' The Butler puts his hands in his hip pockets and rocks backward and forward, heel to toe. 'She's one of Quinn's first. Go on, hit the button; go on.'

Benny reaches forward and presses the slow-release switch.

Lights flash inside the Medusa's body, her organs spin, flowery mammary glands twirl, and the heart pulsates. Every organ Benny can and can't put a name to swirls and flashes in turn, connected to and set off by its adjacent organ, like a game of Mousetrap.

The Butler speaks to the Penny: 'Exposed circuitry is a thing.'

The Penny shrugs. 'Everyone knows that.'

'You mean it's a requested thing?' Benny asks.

'A fetish thing; yes, it's requested.'

'I never knew.' Benny makes a mental note of that little bit of information. It's an excellent idea for the club. He can see it now—the line-up for the Medusa, down the hall, out the doors and into the street.

'This one is a display, Benny. You can't have her,' The Butler states as he moves toward a door behind the Penny.

The Penny smiles. Benny moves past her, following The Butler. He looks back as she switches the fan off, and then switches herself off. Her face collapses, leaving no expression at all. The door slides shut behind them.

The Butler's steps echo forward down the corridor, pinging back at them through the long hallway. A familiar feeling comes over Benny, a feeling he often has when alone in his stock room with nothing but him and the bot stock. He wouldn't name it—especially out loud—but it feels close to fear, born out of uncertainty. He tells no one about it—nobody, not ever.

The walls and ceiling widen, and Benny and The Butler move into a dimly lit, larger space. Benny can't judge the size of the room in the limited light, but the air has changed: it's cooler. A metal platform clangs and echoes under his steps. The sound of thousands of simultaneous movements swirl in the air around him. The Butler flicks a switch, and light floods the factory, showing it to be the size of a sporting oval.

'What you see here, stays here.' The Butler stops to look at him. Benny nods.

Worker bots line the factory floor. The skeletons they work on are larger than normal bots and larger than a human. They whiz in constant motion on transportation tracks. Legs and arms flail with the movement, and they glint in the light, pausing a second at each workstation while adjustments are made and parts attached, melded and connected. A faint whir vibrates in the air. Further along the line, worker bots detail the innards of the robots. Eye sockets follow Benny as he moves on in the wake of The Butler.

'It was Quinn who created the first bot with an accurate and articulated skeleton,' explains The Butler.

'I didn't know,' Benny says.

'Back in the day, he was a celebrity, our Quinn. He appeared on all manner of talk shows.'

Benny shakes his head. He doesn't know these things about Quinn.

The Butler tilts his head back and lets out a stilted chuckle, then switches off the light and pushes through a door, leaving the worker bots to work in the dark. Benny knows all about the limits of bot intelligence, but if that's genuine humour The Butler is displaying, then these service bots are now more advanced than Benny has experienced in the past.

They move further downward, perhaps deeper under the warehouse, past walls lined with shelving and populated with part-built bot parts. It looks like an upright morgue after an unhinged massacre. Benny reaches out and lets his hand waft over their silky skin. They feel like water.

'Quinn tells me you're struggling, Benny.' The Butler tosses this comment casually into the conversation.

'Struggling with what?'

'There's a wider range of uses for bots than you're currently taking advantage of. Open your mind; clients vary widely. Some clients are stricken with loneliness, unable to socialise, and terrified of people and places. Psychiatrists use bots in therapy, parents give them to adult children who struggle with all kinds of challenges, and bored couples acquire them for a bit of safe fun—and that's just the beginning of it. You're not making the most of this large pool of clients.'

They stroll together into a large room that has a plaque over the door indicating The Great Hall. The Butler flails his arms about and recites lists of the potential customers Benny is apparently missing out on. Benny walks at arm's length alongside to avoid The Butler's straying arms. As a child, he longed to be Will Robinson; this, sadly, is as close as he'll get.

'Danger, Will Robinson!' The Butler says, throwing his arms about.

That The Butler has read his thoughts is neither legal nor, Benny thought until now, possible for a service bot. He takes a deep breath and places a hand in his pocket to search for his ear buds to calm the thoughts that have sprung into worries about The Butler's capabilities and unpredictability. After locating them, he puts them in, breathes out and presses the volume button.

The Butler touches a hand to Benny's shoulder to urge him forward. 'So much still to see, Benny; let's keep moving. Lawyers, surgeons,' The Butler says, continuing to list clients he believes Benny should pick up. 'There's a range of illnesses a bot can give comfort to; schools use them in demonstrations, and medical schools make use of the advanced pain sensors. Those bots have sensors in erogenous zones too. They're touchy-feely, those guys.' The Butler's body shivers at the use of the word 'touchy'.

They stop to look up at a series of male robots placed along the wall, which decrease progressively in size in terms of waist flab, starting with a big belly that hangs low, and concurrently increases in abdominal muscle size until, on the last bot, it looks swollen like those of the most advanced body builder. Benny straightens his back and stands taller.

'And there's the curious types,' The Butler says.

They walk past a display of bots labelled by their skin colour: black, red, cream, white, blue, green and orange. Benny pauses before a range of bots in rainbow colours that shimmer with glittering flecks.

'That's the vampire series you're looking at there. The readers demanded the creation of that one.'

'Nice.' Benny nods, admiring the range of hides. He's calmer now, as the range of bots he's seeing gives him hope for his own business.

'The customers felt let down as they had expectations of vampire bots that bite flesh. Which, of course, we gave them initially, but a lawsuit put a stop to that model. Before your time, I think, Benny.'

Benny reaches up and runs his fingers down a thigh. The sparkle is soft to the touch. The shine is deep, embedded, like iridescent jelly. In the darkness of his club, this would be a delight. He'll find a way to have this one. He follows The Butler down the hallway.

'There are collectors who want to own everything, and scientists who study the history of robots. Add to that list the sheikhs, princes and every member of every boy band who's had a low point in their career.'

The range of bots Benny is seeing has his brain firing with excitement. When Quinn warms to assisting him financially in populating the club, the possibilities will be mind-blowing. It can only benefit Quinn to have these in public circulation. Benny's confused as to why Quinn hasn't mentioned them to him before.

'There's so much more I could tell you,' The Butler leans in and whispers, 'Specifically, who ordered what and when, but Quinn values privacy.' He leans away quickly as though the secret is explosive. 'Celebrities like a good time with our bots. They get a friend to do the buying, but they always tell; they always gossip—they can't help themselves.' The Butler grins at the idea of this.

The Butler and Benny walk side by side. Benny pauses on a balcony and looks over a second factory floor. When he was small,

Benny's mother worked a conveyer belt in a chocolate factory. He sat under her bench, cross-legged or sleeping. Occasionally, chocolate bars fell to him like rain; Benny loves factories.

The Butler stops to look at him. 'I'll tell you this. An actor, the one with anger-management issues, purchased five of these old-school issues right here.' He gestures at a glass cabinet that houses old models. 'I saw him on the news, sunbathing with them on his yacht off the coast of Ensenada, and no one knew they were plastics. Most punters take care of business in private, and then hang their bots in the closet, but some desperately want to be seen. Maybe the intrigue of the scandal gives them popularity.'

The features on these bots are familiar: the skin tone, the noses and the wrists. Their features are distinctive to Quinn's work and differ from bots made elsewhere. This is where Benny's therapy bots for his business come from. He can't fathom why Quinn has kept him on basic bots for his business. Clearly, Quinn has never taken him seriously.

The Butler leads him to the end of the hall and presses a code into the lock. 'This,' he says proudly, 'is the 3D-printing room.'

It clearly says 'The Lab' on the door. The Butler waves Benny into the quiet, large room. Benny's eardrums press in on themselves as a result of the soundproofed walls. He turns around and around, gazing at the walls. One wall displays detailed diagrams of the internals of bots, and the rest shelve body parts in orderly groups of torsos, limbs, genitals, heads, bones, facial details and finer details, such as hair. Colourful wires hang like bloodless veins. Two small runner bots dart about before them, stocking the shelves with 3D-produced body parts.

'You can never be in this room unsupervised.' The Butler locks the door they came through. 'But Quinn said you can be trusted.'

'Of course, but I doubt I'd ever be let past the front door without an invitation, would I?' It's a genuine question. Benny would love to be left to wander through the warehouse on his own, but The Butler isn't interested in his questions.

The Butler moves along the wall, closing three doors that open off to the side, which are labelled with tiny plaques and teeny writing. Benny moves in close to peer at them: 'Maternity', 'Paternity' and 'Organics'.

'Are we going in there?' Benny asks.

'There's no access for you, Benny. And may I remind you that what you see in this building stays in this building?'

'What's in there?'

The Butler ignores him. 'This room we're in now is the centre of the entire warehouse. It's the safest room to discuss the details of everything that happens here.'

'It says "Maternity"? Like babies, Butler? Or parents? What's in there?'

'The walls in here are soundproofed and admittance is limited. You're lucky to be here at all, Benny,' The Butler responds, still not answering his questions.

They move through the room. A long table fills the centre. Oddly shaped body parts line the walls: elongated legs, thick arms with multi-joints like extra elbows, small heads and large ears. A chart on the wall details nipple colours and shapes: light red, hot red, pink, chestnut, bronze, peach, orange, tan, brown, black, blue, light blue, cobalt blue, green, yellow and rainbow; and Standard Mini, Mini 1 and 2, Perky, Large Puffy, XL Puffy, XXL Puffy, Super Puffy, Texas Puffy and Big Mama, respectively.

'See Big Mama?' The Butler points toward it. 'She's the largest nipple on record. She's about as big as your fist.'

At the end of the room, The Butler stops. 'Quinn has asked me to convey certain information to you, Benny.'

'Yup.' Benny can feel conditions and let-downs coming. He places his hands on his hips and holds his back tall.

'Quinn said that, for him to invest in your club, he'd like to be confident of its success.'

'Success? I don't see how it can fail, personally.'

Muffled voices come from the maternity room.

Benny nods at it. 'What's that?'

'Quinn believes you need fetish dolls, and to purchase these, you need to bypass the Government Etiquette Key.' The Butler hands him a card.

'You're kidding me? Seriously? He's giving me access to his dolls?'

'Memorise the link on that card. You'll get all you desire from that site. Quinn will give you credit. Order what you need, but there's a limit. If you need to speak to him about this arrangement, come to the front door and tell the Penny you want to see me. Have you memorised the link? Give it back to me.'

Benny looks at the line of garbled letters and numbers that make up the link: http://6c8e2CHA_CHA_Unimatej.ONION/

Benny looks at The Butler. 'May I …?' He motions slipping the card into his pocket.

'No.'

Benny reaches behind his ear and touches a finger to his third dot to take a snap of the card.

The Butler thrusts his hand to cover it. 'No, you can't save it in your personal data; it's vulnerable. It's easier to memorise than you think. Think about it, Benny. Read it slowly' The Butler watches Benny closely.

'Memorised?' The Butler checks.

'Umm … Yep, got it.'

'Good.' The Butler reaches up with a finger and taps-taps him on the forehead. 'Keep it in there. You'll get everything on that site that you're not supposed to. You'll see. There's celebrity look-a-like bots that cater for fetishes. We've got animal behaviour. We've got the range of abuses: you hit me, I'll hit you harder, etcetera, etcetera.

You'll find everything you require to skyrocket your business to where Quinn believes it needs to be.'

The Butler unlocks a door and leads the way across the hanging walkway. Below, hundreds of suspended bodies receive finishing touches. It looks like a silent rave.

'Here's where they add specifics: fingernails, freckles, hair, genitals, breasts and chests, nipples (like those you saw earlier), lips, eyebrows, tattoos, piercings, removable tongues, throats, eyes, fangs and toenails. Thousands of combinations create a unique doll, priced accordingly.'

'All females, Butler?'

'No, Quinn has anything you can imagine. Flaccid and hard penis attachments, dangling testicles'—The Butler waves his arm about to emphasise the range of options—'tight testicles, available in all sizes and skin tones. Hermaphrodite dolls—enthusiasts can be picky! There are those who want the vagina and the penis; those who want the vagina, penis, but no testicles; and others order removable genitals so they can go back and forth between genders. If they've had enough of the penis, they can remove the attachment and put the vagina back in. See this fella here?' The Butler points to one of the alcoves tucked into the back of the walkway. 'Come on,' he says, and together they step into the little cubby hole display. 'The plus-size has been popular with its plump rump and jiggly gel implants. It has a strong, thick waist and heavy, big legs. He's our most voluptuous boy. Hold his nuts, Benny; go on.'

'Naw, I'm good; I can see from here they look like real good nuts.'

'Come on, Benny. You must learn all about what's on offer for your club.'

Benny points a finger and pokes at the soft flesh. 'Not my thing, but yeah, real nice.'

'Come on, give them a real good feel.'

Benny takes one in each hand. 'Feels real enough,' he says quietly.

'Does it? Feel real to you?' The Butler asks. 'Quinn has been working on getting it just right. He's aiming for a natural human feel. He says it's cuddly.'

The Butler moves on down the hallway. He's going fast now, and he leaves Benny behind holding the big nuts. Benny lets the squishy, big sacks fall from his palms and runs a step or two to catch up. The Butler swings open a door, and there's the Penny sitting in the dim light at the desk below the bot with the Medusa dreadlocks.

'And here we are, back at the start, Benny.'

The Butler holds the door open, 'Bye Bye, Benny', he says, and Benny steps through and the door slams heavily behind him. He makes his way back up the corridors and steps out into the bright sunlight, blinking and smiling. The street noise hums. He walks long the footpath and presses his dots to record as he speaks the link to the dark web that The Butler gave him. There's no way he's going to remember all that without assistance.

16

Henry & Dale

Henry holds one arm around the box, and with the other, he presses a finger to the lift button. The doors open, and he gets in and selects his floor. The entire way home in his car, he tilted his head to make room for her—his short, square, cardboard-box date. As the lift ascends, he rubs his cricked neck and stretches from side to side.

The lift stops and opens at his floor. He hugs the box to his side and drags it out. Coming down the hallway toward him, from his apartment, he sees he has a visitor. She moves faster toward him once she sees him, then leans her head to read the side of the box, which—for privacy—is completely bare of any logo or wording. It's just a plain, brown cardboard box—which could possibly tell her everything she wants to know anyway.

'What you got there?' Dale asks.

'Hello.' He shuffles past her, dragging his box with him.

She follows behind, then pauses to lift the end, helping.

'I've got it; I've got it,' he says. 'No help needed.'

They wrestle it together as she rests it back down clumsily on the floor.

'You're a surprise,' he says. 'It's your day off; everything okay?'

'All good. I'm out on an errand. Got time for a coffee?' she asks.

He drags the box down the corridor with Dale walking alongside —an excruciating process. He leans it on the wall beside his front door. The box is shoulder high. He doesn't recall if Vince chose a height or let the automated selections choose for him. Domin must be short—or currently headless.

Still rigid with alarm at Dale's untimely visit, he breathes in deeply, unlocks his front door and lets her in before him. She's upbeat, happy, bouncing on her toes as she steps inside. He follows her inside and pushes the door closed behind them. He spends more time than needed locking his multiple vintage locks. He likes the scrape of the metals as he moves the keys.

Dale, right there beside him, points. 'Your parcel. You left it outside.'

He laughs and begins the process of unlocking the door again.

'Shall I start a coffee?' she asks.

'That'd be nice.'

She saunters away, taking chunks of his anxiety with her. He drags the box inside, lies it behind the couch and then locks the door once more. He hears the kitchen cupboard doors click, click, click as she searches for coffee-making things among the tidy rows of black and white mugs and the cutlery placed with their ends in a perfect line.

'I'll fix the coffee. You be the guest,' he calls out. 'I'll make the best coffee you've ever had.'

'Is that right?'

'It is. I baristad my way through uni,' he says, coming in to the kitchen.

He slides the coffee beans into the grinder. He'll make sure the only thing she'll have on her mind is coffee, coffee, blissful coffee.

'I don't think "baristad" is a word,' she says.

Coffee-making noises halt the conversation. She sits behind him at the breakfast counter. He doesn't yet know her well enough to take a guess at what she's thinking about. He glances at her, smiling. She smiles back at him. The rich scent of coffee rises and drifts about them. He wants to say to Dale he's proud that his coffee beans are locally roasted, but he's not proud of the sinking water table in the desert where these beans are grown. So, he says nothing. He wipes the bench where the brown liquid has dribbled, then he passes a cup to her with both hands, containing the beautiful coffee he's made her.

'You've worked long hours this week,' she observes. 'I thought I'd surprise you with a social visit.'

'They're keeping me busy; there's a lot happening.'

'Changes?'

'Management changes.'

'Does that mean changes for you?' She queries, looking at him over her cup while she sips.

Henry is unsure if Project City is open knowledge in the office. His way of going about things has always been to keep quiet until Quinn speaks openly first. 'There might be changes for me; I really don't know yet, but as soon as I do, you'll know too.' He's so far avoided any conversation about the doll now lying behind his couch, but he's perhaps instead jumped straight into a confidential conversation that he doesn't want to have.

'You know what?' he says. 'This coffee is pretty bad.' He lifts the cup from her hands. She barely lets go, and he tips it down the sink. 'Let's go out for real coffee.'

'I wasn't minding your coffee actually.'

'You're kind, but I *was* minding it.'

He places one palm on her back and ushers her through the loungeroom, past the couch and to the front door, where she watches as he works at unlocking his locks.

Once they've left the apartment and got in the lift, Henry presses the ground-floor button. 'These walls,' he says, and puts his palm to the glass and looks at the floor. The vibrations move through his hands and though his body.

'Anything I can do to help?'

He shakes his head and rolls his eyes at his own inadequacies. The lift slows and comes to a stop at level two. The door opens. Vince is there, grinning back at them.

'Vince? Where you off to?' Henry asks.

Vince wheels himself to the lift door. 'Hey there. Did you pick up what you need?'

Henry loves a good Vince joke normally, but to ask after the doll right in front of Dale isn't funny and, Henry thinks, is even alarming—especially after he'd only just avoided a conversation with Dale about it. Henry puts a foot to Vince's wheel and shoves him back out the door. 'Out you go, mate. No room in here. I'll catch you later.' He pokes at the close button, again and again, until it begins to slide shut.

'Not letting me in?' Vince calls at them. He leans forward as the door closes on his bewildered face.

Dale waves at Vince as he disappears behind the door.

'I think he wanted to come in with us,' she says.

'He's fine. He can wait for it to come back up.'

≈

Dale sits close to Henry in his favourite spot—the corner seat of Café Bang-Bang. She still holds the menu in her hand, reading it.

She rubs her widow's peak where it strains on her forehead, and tiny hairs ping free. Together, they watch the smooth gait of the waitress as she walks away with their order.

'These service dolls are way too perfect,' Henry says. 'Every detail is symmetrical and precise, down to the toenails—it's hard to take them seriously.'

They both glance at her open toe shoes, it's a sign that she's a bot —no human would be allowed to wear open toe shoes in this job.

'I'm not sure "perfect" is the right word to describe it,' Dale says.

They watch the doll move to stand behind the counter. A nearby customer throws a finger in the air, and the doll bounces back to life, smiling with large, white teeth as she rushes forward.

'Fake, then,' Henry says.

'Tell me if I'm wrong,' Dale questions, 'but I think you assume we all want to see bots with flawed bodies of real age, real weight and real skin, right?'

'I haven't thought too much about it to tell you the truth,' he ponders. 'I don't actually have a say in it, so there's no point in my having an opinion, and I don't think Quinn spends a lot of time pondering the perfection of his dolls either,' Henry says. 'It's just the way he wants it. Maybe he should spend more time thinking about it.'

'Maybe he should,' she agrees. 'I suppose if anybody actually took the time to do a study on it, they'd say nobody wants to be looking at perfection and feel like they have to live up to expectations of symmetry and flawlessness—'

'True,' Henry says. 'It's one of the causes of depression, trying to live up to perfect lives and looks on social media, isn't it?'

'—but if you ask me,' Dale continues, 'it's actually the reverse, people don't want to see their imperfections reflected back at them; they don't want to see the reality of weakness and foibles and defects—they find that even more depressing. They want to see their potential. Like Queen Grimhilde in *Snow White and the Seven Dwarfs*—see beauty, not truth; humans want to keep up the pretence that perfection is possible.'

The immaculate bot arrives at their table and slides a coffee to each of them. Henry glances at its skin and imagines how he'd feel if it were pockmarked, and if the bot had jowls and wobbling love-handles. 'I've never thought of it that way,' he says. He doesn't tell her that he thinks he probably wouldn't like a flawed doll—the words *ugly doll* hang around on the tip of his tongue. He wants his Domin to arrive looking like the most symmetrical, streamlined, flaw-free doll possible; and he also doesn't say that he can't figure out why this is the case.

Dale shrugs and taps the table musically with a teaspoon. 'There's also the matter of deception. When you see perfection, you know straight away it's a doll, and you know where you stand with it—what to expect, or not to expect, of it. But if you see reality—overweight and thinning hair, for example—you assume it's human, right?'

'Pretty much.'

'So, if it's a flawed bot, that's deception, right?' Dale shrugs at him as though it's an insolvable conundrum.

He's on the verge of telling her he doesn't see the problem; what difference does it make if you're unaware whether it's a bot or a human? It's kinda fun, even freeing, but then she takes it in a completely different direction.

'If you want to know what I really believe, it's this: for us to really be human, and feel a sense of wholeness about our lives, we need to be with other humans, have real conversations and have genuine feelings, and ditch the interactions with the 1s and 0s altogether. So, we *need* to know if we're speaking to a human or a bot. We need to be in a position to tell the difference, right? Think about the simplest version of this, how do you feel when you're communicating online to, let's say, a complaint service for your internet, and you suddenly realise you've been speaking to a bot, not a human; it's irritating. It doesn't feel like you've been given genuine service.'

Henry's thoughts keep coming back to his Domin, and how he'd like things to be when he opens that box. He decides a change in the direction of the conversation is a good idea. 'Ever thought about going into robotics instead of business?' he asks her.

Dale shakes her head in an adamant no. She shivers dramatically as though the idea disgusts her. 'It's funny you should ask, because it actually used to be my goal—to be a robotics engineer—but things changed for me along the way. The more unreal and uncertain the world has become, the more I yearn for a world of facts.'

Henry nods. He has nothing to add to the conversation. He's mentally going through his day-to-day life wondering where in his life there is uncertainty and lack of facts. And then he thinks about his car, and how much he likes knowing, and seeing, how everything mechanical in it works, and how much he hates the lack of any human element in the self-drives.

'I want to know who I'm talking to,' she continues, 'a bot or not? Am I having a drink in a bar with someone who's an ad? Or just someone who wants to have a drink with me? I want to control what I drive, where I live, and whether I have a baby or not.' Dale pauses and glances at Henry's face, which probably looks blank to her. 'Just walking around minding my own business, I'm bombarded with false ideas, even blatant lies, with the sole aim of manipulating what I do next, what I buy, who I vote for, where I holiday, who my friends are, and even what questions I ask of myself: how I judge myself, my looks and my actions. Consequently, the more intense is my need to engage with authentic actions and thoughts. No, Henry,

I won't be using this internship to get into robotics; I'll be using it to *understand* robotics.'

'Yeah, I wanted to be happy too, once.' Henry laughs. He feels Dale has stated something real to him about who she is; however, she's looking for clear-cut lines and demarcations between everything in her life, but it can't ever be that way anymore. He can't help but believe she'd be a great influence on Quinn; nothing can ever be as clear, and biological, or as true as she'd like it to be, but she'd be a great reality check for QRC.

'I don't know if you've noticed,' he says, 'but Quinn's kind of blinkered in his drive to create his robots.'

'What do you mean?'

Henry gazes out the window at the river. He makes a connection now, that what Dale is speaking about now, is connected to his love of this café; the love of nature outside, the river, the large trees. 'Quinn kind of reminds me of those people who are super intelligent in only one area. Quinn's a genius when it comes to innovation, but emotionally, he's a total moron.'

'Let's just call him what he is,' she says. 'He's a sociopath, right?'

'You're probably right about that.'

'Can I disappoint you even further, Henry? Quinn's actually not as much of a genius as you think. He doesn't get his ideas out of thin air. He takes his cues from his own life and his own body. The base nature of his dolls starts with him; they think the way he does, behave the way he does, and respond the way he does. Little Quinn replicas. His dolls are all sociopaths.'

Henry listens to what Dale has to say, but she can't be right. 'If you're right, Dale, then every single doll out of Quinn's factory would be a sociopath.'

'Yes, and each part of Quinn's dolls is a separate creation; they're 3D-printed pieces with their own dot brain: the arms, necks, legs, heads, fingers—everything. Each little piece has its own model of Quinn's quirks and abilities—or disabilities—or mental state. Do you understand what I'm telling you, Henry?'

'I get what you're saying, but since almost every doll in this town comes out of Quinn's warehouse, and as his advanced dolls begin to roll out into projects, that would mean there would be a lot of Quinn-like sociopaths in the population.'

Dale shrugs at him.

He expected her to explain where his thinking had gone wrong, and tell him, "No, this is not true", but she nods as if to say, "Yes, it's all true, but what's to be done about it?"

17

Henry, Vince & Domin

Henry pokes a pair of scissors under the zip tie and snips. One of Domin's pale limbs falls to the floor. Thud. He looks around the room. He imagines that moments like this—putting together your first doll—don't go unnoticed by the walls.

A whistle of breeze finds its way to his cheeks from the open louvres. Henry holds her right arm by the wrist. His fingers encircle her soft skin. He snips this free too and places it on the floor beside her first arm. He releases a leg, and it falls to the floor, bent backwards: in a gangly heap, as if she's passed out after a heavy night. Then, he does the same for her other leg, torso and head. She's a girl segmented and bubble-wrapped: arms, legs, torso, head, and, perhaps an invisible segment? Her soul? He flips her torso over. It feels improper. Smiling at her, he says her name: 'Domin.' It's comforting to say her name and smile at her; it gives him permission to manipulate her this way.

Henry didn't expect her to come with paper instructions. He slips them into his pocket. He likes to think he's acquired his very own human, and as a human, there's no need for instructions. He picks

122

up an arm and lets it drop to the floor again. She's heavier than he expected. Her fingers are curled into a fist. He puts his fingertips to hers. She has a silken touch. No fingerprints. He takes her fingers in his own and straightens them out, and again, like the closing of a petal, they crawl, slowly, back to her palm into a loose fist.

He goes into the kitchen. The boiling water hisses at him. He glances back at her through the doorway. She looks like a crime scene. He stands at the kitchen window and watches the towering buildings shimmer in the distance. In the foreground, the drone activity is thick. He closes the louvres. The apartment is cool, and private.

He takes his coffee back to her and he sits on the floor with her parts scattered about him, and her head propped up on his knees. He unwinds the bubble wrap from her face, around and around and around, while her head flips in his lap. He rests the head on the floor, and in one quick move, strips the bubble wrap from her neck like a Band-Aid. Unlike the basic models, she has tiny pores that are empty, black pinholes.

With the app, he checks Domin's connections. Darkened squares positioned at her seams glow, giving a virtual thumbs up after he makes each connection. Her parts glide together, her joins seamless. He moves slowly and pays close attention until all but her head are connected. He lays her out, steps back and looks. He admits he's afraid of this pleasant-to-the-eye Frankenstein creature, this fooler of sorts.

He places her headless body on the couch; her legs hang, bending at the knee joints. Her small feet rest lightly on the floor. Henry doesn't know why this quiet resting of her feet should unnerve him. He takes her hands in his and places them together in her lap. He sits next to her, with her body on one side of him and her head on the other side. He holds a coffee in one hand and rests his other hand on his lap.

There's a knock at the door. Henry rolls Domin off the couch and tucks her underneath it, poking her arms and feet out of sight. He drops her head into the box and shuts the lid.

'What's wrong?' Vince asks when Henry opens the door.

'Nothing's wrong.'

'Nothing? I'm not great at social etiquettes, but I'm thinking when you open the door to someone it's normal to speak, you know; something like, "Hello Vince."'

'Hello Vince,' he says.

'Can I come in?'

Henry takes a step back and holds the door open wide. Vince wheels himself in and leans back to shut the door. They stand there, looking at each other. Vince grins. Henry fakes calm.

'What?' asks Vince.

'You want a beer? I need a beer.' Henry heads for the kitchen.

'Bit early, isn't it?'

Vince's wheels squeal on the flooring as he follows behind Henry. 'Is that box what I think it is?' he probes, rubbing his hands together.

Henry isn't ready to be excited about the doll. He kinda resents Vince's intrusion. It's not Vince's excitement to have. They've shared a lot of strange hobbies in their long friendship together: usually honest plastic, like Lego, trains and Meccano. They even had a stint of paper-doll obsessions for a while. However, they were all different to this—there was no shame in those things, for the most past, anyway.

'Where is she, Hen? Where ever is your new friend?' Vince spins on his wheels and pushes off to the bedroom. Then, he's back and en route to the bathroom. 'Where is she, Henry?' he calls. 'Remind me, is she the same as mine?' A cupboard opens and shuts, then Vince appears back in the kitchen. 'They can be friends. That'd be a hoot.'

'Stop it.' Henry pushes a beer at him.

'Where've you hidden her?'

'There's nothing to see. She's the same as yours.'

'Although, I expect mine's older, worse for wear. Is she in here?' He moves around the couch and laughs. 'Oh, there … there she is.' Vince leans forward and calls, 'Hello, hello? Is she on? What's she doing under there all on her lonesome?'

'I'm still reading the instructions.'

'When have you ever needed instructions? Get her out, and let's have a good squiz at her. I'll get her going for you.'

'Will she think she's yours if you're the one to start her up?'

'She's not a duck. Get her out from under the couch. She'll suffocate. She needs to be upright to breathe.'

Henry rushes forward and drags her out, tugging her by her waist.

Vince laughs. 'Joke, mate.'

He pulls her up on to the couch and stands back beside Vince to look at her.

'She's nice,' Vince says. 'I think she's chunkier than mine. Did we specify a size?'

Henry crosses his arms. He glances at Vince, then back at his doll being judged by Vince.

'I can't remember if we chose her size,' Vince ponders. 'It was certainly an option. Do you like her?'

Henry leans forward and places her ankles together and her hands on her thighs. He pulls her head out from the box and sits it in her lap.

'Wait until you rev her up. She'll be realer than real when she lights up. Here, look, pass me her head.' Vince grabs her head by the hair and rips the last of the plastic from her eye lids. With finger-nails and concentration, he picks the plastic from the end of each of four tubes that hang from her neck. 'Watch this, Hen.' He slips his finger inside Domin's neck, and with his eyes upward to the ceiling, feels around. 'Stick your finger in there and hold down that bump.'

Henry slides his fingers inside her neck. It's soft, and giving, like dough. He has a vision of his father's butcher business, with animal carcasses hanging by thick hooks in the cool room. He finds a knuckle-like bump and pushes it. It clicks under her skin, but nothing happens.

Vince takes her head and hovers it over the neck of her body. 'Watch.' He lowers the head to the neck. The wires draw up and connect, each wire sounding off—ding, ding, ding, ding. The skin of her neck and head melds seamlessly. Vince grabs her by the wrist and rips the plastic off her fingers and toes. She bumps around on the couch like a bag of fruit.

Henry can't picture how this floppy, plastic body could ever help him with his problem. This is the first time he's allowed this connection to occur in his thoughts. She's supposed to be his remedy, his medicine, his balm. According to Benny, she's his therapy.

'Put her address and details in here.' Vince holds back her hair and taps on the back of her neck with two fingers. A square patch of skin becomes translucent.

'This is how you deactivate her, if you need to.' Vince glances at Henry. 'Seriously, you might need to, so just give a double tap right here.'

'Vince, what do I do about her if she just up and leaves me?'

'She won't. She'll know her location. You'll put it in when we set her up. You own her. She's yours, and she knows it. If she happens to go out alone or she's stolen, she'll come straight home like a cat.' Vince looks at Henry. 'Don't be scared of her. She's your new toy. It's Christmas. Unwrap and enjoy.'

The new toy lies on his couch, twisted, face down and with one leg awkwardly under the other, like a puppet. He's disgusted at the idea and disgusted in himself. He watches Vince all over it as though it's the best thing to ever happen.

Vince turns her over and brings her rear to his lap, and with one hand lassoing in the air, he shouts, '*Woo-hoo!* and bounces her about. '*Mate! She's an upgrade from mine! Woo-hoo! Her hips are so soft! I gotta get me one of these!*

'Really, Vince?' Henry grabs her by her limp hand, whisks her from her ordeal in Vince's lap and puts her back on the couch. 'Do you have to?' He arranges her again with her ankles together and hands in her lap.

'Oh, I get it. Sure, mate, that's okay. You want to believe in the whole story.' Vince pats his arm patronisingly. 'She's your new best friend.'

Henry feels the need to explain to Vince how he's thinking about his new bot. He doesn't know how to, or even if he should, tell Vince about Dale's belief that these dolls are versions of Quinn, with all Quinn's imperfections. He's going to have to block that idea out.

Vince leans off his chair and nudges Henry. 'Let's get her set up for you. Come here; you set her up. I'll tell you how.'

Henry moves in beside him, wanting to get it done so this nightmare can be over.

'Man, once you get her operational, she'll be like your real-time girlfriend, especially if you're going for the whole emotion settings. You will, right, since you're into that? But whatever you do, don't allow her internet access. Once we've set her up, we'll activate the internet blocker. That'll shut her up, otherwise she'll start getting ideas and creating lists of things for you to get for her.'

'But once she's operating and real, I should let her do what she wants, right?'

Vince shrugs. 'It's up to you. Dicey, though. See that grid there? That's where you punch the details in. She won't come on until you answer the questions that'll pop up on her grid. Yeah, that's it. Now wait for the first question. What's it say?'

'Address.'

'Yeah, so put that in. See, now she'll know where she lives. She'll always come back to you, like a homing pigeon. You're her big daddy pigeon.' Vince chuckles.

Henry presses in his address.

'Hey, did you get your keys back from Dale?' Vince asks, while watching over Henry's shoulder and breathing beer breath on him. 'You still want me to keep a set of keys for you or are they Dale's now? Is she moving in? Have you discussed, you know, Domin with her? That'll be weird.' Vince gives a snort.

'It's asking me to name her, Vince.'

'So, give her a name, buddy. Be a god now, name the queen of your harem.'

Henry touches the keys to type in the name he'd been mulling over for days. 'Of course, Dale's not moving in. Why would you even say that? Don't you have my spare keys?' Henry stops typing to look at Vince.

'The keys Dale took. Quick, put her new name in before it moves on to the next question. It's complicated to go back and change it. Think of a name you won't mind saying over and over again; you know, over and over and over and over and—'

'What key did Dale take?'

'Your house key. I gave it to her the other day. I saw you with her in the lift afterwards. You shut the lift door on me because you're a selfish arsehole.'

'Yep, that was really thoughtful of you, Vince.'

'What was? You're being sarcastic. What have I done now?'

'You asked me if I'd picked up the doll from the post office right in front of Dale. You knew I didn't want anyone knowing about this.' He points a finger at Vince's forehead. 'Don't even talk about it in your sleep.'

'Okay, but no, I didn't say anything in front of Dale. I wouldn't tell a soul. It's between you and me. Our dirty little secret.' Vince laughs, and he pokes his finger at him, in his ribs, his ear and in his hair.

'Yes, you did.' Henry slaps at Vince's fingers. 'You said, "Did you pick up what you need?"'

'No, I … no, I was speaking to Dale, not you.'

Henry watches the screen accept the name he's chosen. He wonders if she'll like it or reject it. Can it do that? Can it reject choices he's made for it?

'Dale knocked on my door that day,' Vince explains. 'She said you'd asked her to borrow your key from me so she could get into your apartment to collect documents for the office. And then I saw you both in the lift, and I asked—'

'Yeah, you asked her if she picked up what she needed.'

'Yep. With me now?'

'Yes, I'm with you now. I thought you were asking me if I'd picked up this doll. Only, I never asked Dale to borrow my keys from you. She was at my door that day when I got home from the post office.'

'Geez, mate, best you get to the bottom of that one.'

It's something he might do—ask Dale to go to Vince's house for his spare key—but he didn't. It didn't happen.

Vince watches his face. 'Should you be trusting her? You're kind of backward about things, Henry; you keep a lot of non-digitised paperwork in your place.'

'I like paper. Anyway, she's okay; she's cool.'

'How long have you known her?'

'I know her well enough to know she's a good person.' Henry's first impression of Dale came about the day he witnessed her help a woman struck down by a self-drive. He's seen it before, most people don't help. They don't want to get involved. But Dale, she was right in there by the woman's side. 'And yeah, I forgot; I did ask her to get my keys from you,' Henry lies. 'I asked her to pick up some papers, sorry.'

'Okay. You're a big boy. You know what you're doing. What did you name her?'

'Viv.'

'What?'

'I've named her Viv, short for Vivify. It means to give life to,' Henry clarifies.

Vince stares back at him. 'Well, I think you've overthought that, mate. I can't imagine it: "Give it to me, Viv"; "Bend over, Viv"; or, "Oh, oh, oh, Viv." Doesn't work for me, Hen, but whatever floats your boat. Let's get her lively then.'

The cuckoo jumps out at them and announces the time with its door-slap and squawk.

'Jesus! You need to get rid of that thing. It's a monster.'

'It's kind of grown on me. Okay, so it's four-fifteen, and we're late for an appointment that's in twenty minutes, you and me,' says Henry. 'Can we leave this for now? Will it be okay? How do we pause it?'

Vince taps the grid on her neck, and the whites of her eyes go black.

18

Henry, Vince & Scottie

The psychologist's office at Fuennel Industries is tucked away in the basement of a decommissioned dental school. Henry's memory of it is that it was to be demolished, but it was saved at the last minute and lovingly repurposed by Scottie Fuennel.

The local media made a point of emphasising the town's excitement over Scottie's renovation endeavours. As a cyborg engineer who repairs and enhances failing bodies, they expected miracles: "We look forward to following Dr Fuennel's journey as she lovingly salvages and enhances our town's decrepit building, and we hope this won't be her only escapade in the reconstruction industry. If anyone respects the difference between a worthwhile salvage and rot, it's our Dr Fuennel."

Henry is quietly grateful for this. He loves these old buildings. The sliding door wakes its old bones to let them through, clunking and wiggling as Vince shoves his chair and glides through the doorway, hitting a seam in the old linoleum, where his wheels jam, his chair lurches—and turfs him out to land flat onto his stomach on the floor.

'Jesus!' Henry runs forward, and crouches down to look into Vince's face.

Vince is laughing. 'What an entrance,' he says.

'You, okay? Are you hurt?'

'Don't think so—lucky I'm fat. Help me up.'

Vince pushes himself up, and Henry, uselessly, guides him back into his chair.

'What'd you do that for?' Henry asks, laughing.

Vince sniggers, 'Is that a bad omen? Should we turn around and leave?'

'Easy does it, we're still going in.' Henry gives his chair a shove with his foot, and they move on through the building.

Overhead signs show them the way through the narrow corridors to an area where well-lit offices dressed in modern decor branch off here and there, renewing Henry's confidence in bringing Vince here. Staff sit at desks in spacious communal areas, huddled in discussion. It's quiet. Not uneventful, but peaceful, with less of the angst of the foyer.

Henry's footsteps echo about the foyer, bringing back to them an aura of angst from the ghosts of unsettled dental patients. They follow the signs through long, narrow corridors and arrive at a large counter that cuts across a circular waiting room, beyond which sits a grinning greeter with square teeth and Vince's name on her tongue. Henry stands back while Vince engages in some banter; he watches him straighten his back, square his shoulders and share his range of smiles while she speaks. Vince loves human services. For him, it's a hobby.

'I guess I'll be taking a seat then,' Vince says, waving his arm dramatically across the room.

Henry looks at the field-green armchairs that cosy up to the curve in the circular walls. 'Shall we try these chairs, Vince?'

Henry takes a seat, and Vince sits in another, his wheelchair beside him. With the vibration mode switched up to eleven, Vince lies back and smiles. 'This'll be good for the twinge in my back I just gave myself with that impressive face plant,' he says.

The air temperature in the room is on the cool side, enough to dry sweaty patches. The chairs are angled like sun loungers, creating a comfortable but vulnerable tone. Henry shuns thoughts that lean toward the possible outcomes of placing himself at the mercy of Scottie Fuennel and her psychologist.

'I'll come in with you,' Henry offers.

'I do love your company, Henry, but this time, no—just no; you will not come in with me.'

Henry leans back in his chair and finds a sweet spot where the massager presses into his back. 'This whole place has been a no-go zone for me,' he whispers. 'Since way back when I started with Quinn, I've been itching to get inside and see this show.'

'Why haven't you? All you need to do is walk in the front door, like we just did, and wander around until you're told you can't. What can they do, throw you out?' Vince shrugs.

'Well, technically, I have been in here, but I haven't physically been in this building.'

Vince raises his eyebrows at Henry and nods toward the greeter to suggest this isn't the right place to admit trespass, and he's right, but it doesn't stop Vince going ahead and talking about Scottie and Quinn.

'They have a combative history, don't they? Quinn and Scottie; a nasty business.' Vince closes his eyes. 'I'm gonna get me one of these massagers.'

'I'd say it's more a difference of passions.'

'Have you followed their wrangling online? That's not a difference of passions; that's a cage fight.'

'It's a discussion, Vince. They stand for different ideals. Their problem is they both believe it's a black-and-white field. Look at us taking advantage of Scottie's cybotic services, and at the same time, I'm about to head up Quinn's city of robots; if you ask me, they sit comfortably side by side.'

'A city of robots,' Vince says dreamily. 'What could go wrong there?'

A patter of footsteps moves toward them, and a squat woman appears in the doorway. She owns a smile as wide as her face and a body as wide as the corridor. Her white uniform absorbs the forest colours of the walls and chairs around them, and she glows fluoro-green.

'Vince?' she asks.

'Now there's a face I can trust,' Vince responds, the truth abandoned in the pursuit of an alliance. He climbs into his chair and pushes off to follow her.

They disappear to the sound of Vince's nervous chatter and the slip, slip, slip of her sneaky shoes that go on and on down the hallway until Henry can't tell if he can still hear them or he's imagining them.

≈

Henry isn't surprised to see Scottie enter the waiting room. She comes to him from a separate corridor, loping casually and bringing a large familiar smile with her.

'Hello Henry.' She folds her heavy skirt beneath her and sits on the armrest of the chair Vince vacated, and possibly remembering Henry's passion for good coffee, she hands him a sweet-scented brew.

'Scottie herself,' he says. He's pleased to see her, even though he's certain there'll be manipulation in play at some point—at most, bribes or blackmail, and at least, mocking or praise—to coax him into revealing or agreeing to something. He expects nothing less of Scottie, and he'd be disappointed if she didn't respect his position enough to try something on.

'You didn't think I'd let this opportunity pass, did you? What with you caught like a rabbit in my own territory.'

He takes the coffee. 'No, I didn't, but bearing coffee is an unexpected treat. You won't share this little adventure of mine with Quinn?'

She laughs. She thinks he's joking. 'We have a deal, correct? You're meeting with our psychologist after Vince?'

'We have a deal.' Henry nods. But he has plans that this appointment will be a short and sweet meeting of no consequence. He will not speak of his medical problems, and this will be the one and only appointment. There will be no joy here for Scottie.

'This is a good thing you're doing for your friend.'

'We'll see. I hope he keeps an open mind. He says he wants to stay clean.'

'Clean?'

'Clean of enhancement—pure human. "Cyborgs are for the movies." Is his favourite saying.'

'Fat chance of that,' she says. 'Not a single one of us is pure human anymore. If he's been anywhere near a GP lately, he'll have cybology working away inside him without even knowing it. We all do.'

'He'd freak if you told him that.'

She laughs. 'You don't discuss your work with him then?'

People assume Henry understands a lot about robotics, and that working under Quinn automatically makes him a roboticist. He *should* know more than he does, but his title is Quinn's business manager. He's a salesman, lobbyist and debt collector. He woos politicians to let things through, and attracts businesses to invest or buy, or to update their bots—basically, he's an admin guy. He lets people believe he's across everything in Quinn's realm, because it's useful. Henry keeps Scottie talking. He'd love to get a hint of what she expects to gain from his appointment today.

'You two, you and Quinn,' he says, 'why don't you work together? You've got a wealth of expertise between you. You'd do amazing things if you combined efforts.'

'You know better than that, Henry.' She fakes being aghast with her long eyebrows pointing upward. 'Let me tell you something. When Quinn and I studied robotics back in the day, there was a study done by a women's studies group. I didn't give much time to it then. I envied the barefoot girls, but I was really only ever about the science, though I did fill out a questionnaire for them. I was flippant: tick, tick, tick. As a courtesy, they gave us the results of that questionnaire, and my life changed then and there.'

Henry presses the side button of the chair and raises it upright. With Scottie talking over him like this, he'd begun to feel inferior. 'I remember you. Straight up science, a steel rod. You were angry at being made to do compulsory economics with soft-footed guys like me.' He laughs.

She smiles at this. 'I mean, everything became clear to me then. I think most students shoved the results of that questionnaire in the trash and forgot about it. And I don't know why, but I read it. We all find our passion eventually, don't we? That is, if we're open to it, and that day I decided what I'd do with the rest of my life.'

Henry sips his coffee. It's great coffee. He wonders when might be a good time to interrupt her and ask where she got it.

'The study pointed out that the majority of students taking robotics courses were male. I wasn't surprised by that—and neither will you be, Henry—but the interesting thing it also showed was that, within robotics, males are more interested in the creation of robots in the image of humans, and female students are interested in robotics for cyborg enhancements to improve the human body. It was clear that the future of robotics was in the hands of men who weren't interested in cybotic work, but who wish to create robotic versions of humans, and as it turns out, mostly robotic versions of themselves.'

'I understand what you're saying, but why work against Quinn when you could work with him? You're all about preserving humanity, and so is he. A long and healthy life for everyone. You with your cyborg enhancement procedures, and Quinn with his service robots that do and be everything for us, freeing up our time. Ultimately, you two want the same things.'

'We are *not* the same. There's collateral damage in what he does. Quinn creates slaves, and that's all he aims for. You can't create a meaningful and humane future without considering what you've left in your wake. Quinn doesn't know about the word "humane"; it doesn't exist for him. He wants an intelligent being that does what it's told, and he wants to be known as a hero for his efforts, and that's all.'

'That's one way of looking at it, Scottie, but he has a long-term plan. He's a creative more than he's a scientist. He's an advocate for advanced robots that do complex tasks to free up time for humans. We'd all rather spend our time on meaningful pursuits or be confident that work is being done to the highest possible standards, right?'

'Creative? Quinn? Every one of his robot slaves that I've en-countered identifies as female. There's nothing creative about that. That's another issue he's leading the way with right there: gender stereotypes. He has an opportunity to make a change here, and what does he do? The same old shit: slavery and gender inequality.'

'He's a big believer in creativity, Scottie. He's creating amazing robots. I mean, you two together could be explosive. Robots are far more reliable than humans as carers for the elderly, infirm and children. They don't judge, they don't get tired, and they don't forget medications.'

'Robots for the elderly? How about a nice human hug for the elderly?'

Henry glances at her. He's struggling to imagine Scottie and hugs. 'This Project City Quinn's creating is revolutionary. He has a practicality about our future that makes sense; it's a gift.'

'Gift?' Scottie scoffs. 'We're not talking about the same thing, Henry. Let me put it this way. Over in the QRC warehouse, they're busy making the most intelligent robot we've seen yet, and you should be concerned about what that robot will be capable of—believe me, it's no gift.'

'Are they?' This is news to Henry.

'This is a being more intelligent than you, me and Quinn put together. With its skills in communication, vision and emotion, plus its dexterity, hearing and movement—it's something you and I can never fathom.'

'Okay,' Henry says, trying to imagine this being he's supposed to know about. He wonders if Scottie is concocting this information just to influence him.

'And it thinks differently to us. It doesn't concern itself with the same issues we're concerned about. Us humans will spend time contemplating it, and what it means for it to exist, and we think we might relate to it, but it won't think about us for one second. And what is Quinn doing with these new beings he's created? Using them as sex slaves. Henry, think about it. What does this say about the human race that we create an unprecedented being and task it with being a slave? This isn't advancement or creativity or preserving humanity. This is regression, abuse and selfishness. Haven't we been here before? Think about it. He's got a slave factory going on over there.'

Henry sips at his coffee. It's hot, the way he loves it. He's never been in Quinn's warehouse. 'I think you misunderstand Quinn's intentions.' But as Henry says this, he's not confident he's right, and he's not clear on what a super-being would be used for anyway. More chess?

'I can't allow it, Henry. Will you allow it?'

Henry stands up and wanders to the window. There's a court-yard outside with sandy pathways winding between jacaranda trees, ghost gums and fruit trees with small birds darting between the branches. He looks down the corridor that Vince went down, hoping to see his friendly face. It occurs to him that, while he works closely with Quinn, he's never a party to the details, and so far, he's never really cared. He does what he's supposed to do, and that's it.

'I'll tell you what I'll do, Scottie. I'll make a point of getting to know more about these details of QRC that have so far passed me by.'

'From what I hear, Henry, you're about to head up the biggest slave community in history, so I'm shocked you aren't across all this.'

'You know about Project City? I don't think you can call it a slave city; that's a bit cavalier. I think you might be under the spell of your own ideals, Scottie.'

'If I were you, Henry, I'd make it my job to know what you're getting into. You've been with Quinn, what? Six years? You're a representative of a company you appear to know nothing about. You're just another one of Quinn's puppets.'

'Ten years. It's not my job to question Quinn's work. I know all I need to know. To tell you the truth, I'm pretty much in awe of what he achieves. When Quinn tells me to pass on to our clients that we can upgrade them with a robot that can now take instruction on all manner of difficult and dangerous work, I'm proud of that, and our clients are excited. Nobody cares if they identify as female;

in fact, they find it a relief that a robot can be non-threatening in appearance. Does anybody really care if robots are female?'

'I *bet* they find it a relief. Just because the ability to create something is awe-inspiring, it doesn't mean it should exist. His hero ego will be the ruin of us all. I tell you what, Henry, I'll look after your friend Vince, and I'll look after him well. I'll give him the best, and I'll do it for free if you do this one thing for me: dig into Quinn's work in more detail, and then come back and see me. I'll show you what's going on in my part of the world, and we'll see if you don't change sides real quick.' Scottie stands up and puts her hand out. 'Deal?'

Henry holds his coffee against his chest and puts his free hand deep into his pocket. 'I can't make any deals with you, Scott, but I'll keep a line open to you. We'll talk again. I don't believe there are sides to take here. I still think it'd be a great thing if you worked together.'

Her hand drops. 'Talk is good. I can live with that.'

Scottie watches him lift his cup and drink the dregs of his coffee. 'I'll hold you to it,' she says, 'and just to show you the amazing state of our enhancement work here, I've slipped a pleasant little something-something in your coffee to help you out with your day-to-day life.'

Scottie leaves the same way she arrived: quickly, with a confident stride. Before she's out of sight, she stops to look back at him and smiles. He takes this to be a sign that she joked about the coffee. She would do that. Then, she's gone.

Henry holds his coffee up to the light. It was a pretty good coffee. It's empty, with not a drop left. He smiles into his cup. He breathes it in deeply. Of course, she was joking. She wouldn't do that without his permission.

19

Henry, Viv, & Vince

(Trigger Warning for Sexual Violence)

Vivify is awake.

'What now?' Henry asks of Vince.

It sits on the couch, upright, all limbs and features in place, eyes bright and skin luminescent, looking altogether vibrant. Henry can see now that it's so much more than a remedy. It's a being with a whole lot of vim and aura, and he's damn scared of it.

'Talk to it; it's yours.' Vince places a hand on Henry's arm and pats him with encouragement. 'The beauty of this, Henry, is that you can do to it, with it, at it or on it—if that's your thing—whatever you like. This is … How can I say it? Reaching in deep and hauling out those hushed desires. You know the ones, right? You know what I'm saying. This is where you find out who you really are and what it is you really need. And do you know what the best part is? It's all done without judgement.'

Vince appears to enjoy leading this adventure. Henry gets it. Vince doesn't often have the opportunity to return the friendship favour. Henry would love to be experiencing this with equal enthusiasm, but fresh in his thoughts are Scottie's comments on slavery. And is this—here, in front of him right now—slavery?

'Hello, I'm pleased to finally meet you,' Vivify announces.

Henry takes two steps back. Where there were two, now there are three. The concept isn't new to him. His work is often touched with conversations about the business of this very moment; the realisation that space must be made, physical and mental space, for the idea of a different kind of being. But this, his very own physical experience, has him quite a bit shaken.

'What have you done to it? Mine isn't friendly like this.' Vince wheels forward and peers into its eyes. 'Mine's a bit of a skank really; no manners at all.'

Henry shrugs. 'I chose a high etiquette setting. That could be it.'

Vivify raises one hand slowly, extends two fingers to point at Vince's face, and darting her fingers forward at him, she mimics poking him in both his eyes. Vince jolts backward.

Vivify's mouth opens, and she laughs, loudly.

'High humour setting also,' Henry confirms.

'Is that right?' Vince directs his question to Vivify.

Without any switch in tone in response to Vince's questioning, Vivify answers, 'I like a bit of fun, yes, but manners are important. Diplomacy also, so don't expect me to insult your vulgarity. Which one of you is Henry?'

Vince points.

Henry feels a need to discuss Vivify, to nut it out and to bring this moment to a place of making sense. 'It's a kind of presence, isn't it? I mean—'

Vince looks sideways at Henry. 'No, no, no, Henry; don't go there. Take it for what it is—a plastic doll. A supremely intricate plastic doll.'

Henry winces. 'But what is it? I know it's not the same as us, but this is what makes it equal, right? The appearance of being like us?'

Vince squints at him. 'Philosophy-free zone here, Henry.'

'Scottie believes they're slaves.'

Vince rolls his eyes. 'It's not a slave; it's a man-made doll.'

'Yes, but isn't there a saying: "We see things not as they are, but as we are." How I experience this is how it is. Or how she is.'

'Who said that?'

'A gazillion people.'

'Well, it must be true then,' Vince laughs. 'Henry, right now, you're viewing it as your best friend, right? So, if I were you, I wouldn't spare another thought to it.'

'But it thinks and it feels, and right now I'm very aware of that point. And if I understand that it's a thinking, feeling being, then her even being here in front of me doing as I ask, as my possession, is slavery, right?'

'It's a doll. It's an it; that's what it is. It's not a she. Don't over-think it. There's no blood, no oxygen, no nerves and no thinking, not in our sense of the word anyway. It's just connections, just wires. It might tell you something hurts—and believe me, it will, but it's based on sensing technology—pressure, heat and all that stuff. It's not real, Henry. If I'd known you'd be cray-cray about it all, I wouldn't have bought it for you.' Vince turns on his wheels. 'It's nice to meet you Viv, but it's time for me to leave you and Henry to get to know each other better.'

Henry follows Vince and sticks close to him as he retreats to the door. 'I'm coming down to your place for a while. I need to think this through.'

'Henry, no.' The redness of Vince's boozy skin becomes wilder as he grins. 'Go back in there and play with it. Have a nice little time.'

'I don't think you should leave me alone with her.'

'It's yours, Henry, so best you get to know it. Go on, off you go. The more time you spend with it, the more it'll learn how to please you—you know that, right? It'll become attuned to you alone. It'll be your toy tweaked to your requirements. I expect a full report.'

'A full report?' Vivify queries from the couch. 'I don't think so.' She lifts her right hand and slides hair behind her ear in a smooth movement. The lack of haphazardness in her arm, matched with her clear comprehension of the situation, unnerves Henry a little bit.

'Don't tell me you set the personal rights setting high too?' asks Vince.

'Didn't you with yours?'

'Henry, you're a fool.'

Vivify chuckles. 'Nice to meet you, Vince.' She gives Vince an exaggerated wink, using her whole head in a big nod. 'You're sure you won't stay a while?'

'You might want to rethink those settings, Hen. Don't blame me if you lose control of it.' Vince opens the door.

'See,' Henry calls through the doorway, 'you can only lose control of something if it's real.'

Vince responds, 'Your car, Henry; your car isn't real, and you've lost control of that plenty of times!'

'Don't go; stay and chat with us, Vince,' Vivify requests.

'You're on your own with that one.' Vince flings the door shut.

Viv looks back over the couch at Henry. It occurs to him that there's a predictability in the silent behaviours humans have evolved to agree on—in movements, words, attitudes and thoughts—that don't exist with a robot. The absence of this predictability is disquieting. She's alien-like and unpredictable. He doesn't know what she might do next.

Henry takes a seat on the edge of the couch next to her.

'Henry, if you'd like to change my settings, you can reach behind me, double tap and choose C for change. I'll go through the selections for you again.' She crosses her legs, left over right.

'It's fine,' he says.

That he's programmed her personality to suit himself gives over to a rising feeling of self-consciousness; she's a reflection of his own requirements. Is this what Dale meant when she said the bots were built in the image of Quinn? He's coming close to saying it's a dislike for himself that he's feeling, but he's paid a lot of money to feel this way. She'll complete the job he's bought her to do, or not, and then he'll be rid of her. He thought he might like her. He doesn't.

'I think you've created the perfect grouping of settings, if I may say so myself—but I would, wouldn't I?' She smiles.

Vivify reminds Henry of Esther. Her voice is familiar. It's possible Quinn draws inspiration from the people around him. He doesn't believe for a second Dale's notion that all Quinn's dolls are derived from Quinn's own narcissistic personality, but the idea that Quinn would draw on the people around him is a plausible one.

'You're nervous,' Viv observes. 'Shall we have a drink?'

'What would you like to drink?'

'Anything you'd like, Henry.'

'The same as me?'

'Yes, the same. We're compatible, Henry. You skipped steps during my set-up, so I've chosen to match you in most markers: likes and dislikes, emotional intelligence, humour, belief systems and intelligence quotient. We should get along well. We're similar.'

'You know my IQ?'

'I retain facts about you in my cellular sensor.'

'You've studied my cells?' The panic rollercoaster begins its climb again.

'It's how I know how best to serve you.'

'My cells?' he repeats. He skipped through most of the set-up details. It was too much to take in. He chose the auto-settings made available to him through the set-up, as suggested by those he assumes know better than he does. He imagines explaining this to Vince—or Esther. They'd think him careless.

'It ensures I respect you, Henry. I moderate my intelligence. I guarantee you'll always be more knowledgeable than me. This means I come close to reading your mind. These sayings are vague. I'm wrong; I don't come close to reading your mind ... I read your mind.'

Henry leans in close to Vivify, double taps her neck and presses the C tab.

'Oh,' she laughs, 'something not to your liking? It's the reading-your-mind scenario, isn't it? Before you alter that, I think I can help you. You're confused about how to couple with me. I'm your property, Henry. You do with me what you choose to do. Take my hand and lead me anywhere. My settings ensure no resistance.'

'Couple?'

'You may choose your preferred language terms in my settings. I have regional idioms and colloquial expressions in my vocabulary. You have an option to make me robotic in my expressions—that is, full and clear words appropriate to their meaning, no contractions or slang—or you may leave me at the current selection of semi-formal language. And of course, you may choose accents or languages. The most often selected is French.'

Henry slides through the selections. The 'cellular sensor on/off' message appears, and he selects 'off'. He wants this process he's muddling through with Vivify to be simple, without thought. The need to study her settings brings him too close to examining what he's done by purchasing her. He finds it deceitful that she can mask her manufactured speech with common language. He is reminded of his conversation with Dale about deceit. The robot language setting would serve as a clear reminder of what she is. There's nothing to guide his behaviour here, no manual, and he finds himself wishing it could be somewhere near appropriate to ask Scottie for guidance. Of all people, Scottie could articulate the right way to go about this. How should he treat Viv? As a human? As a robot? Like an appliance? But Scottie has clear boundaries regarding social bots—the conversation would be ridiculous.

'My cellular sensor is off,' Viv confirms. 'May I get you a drink, Henry? I'd like one.'

She touches his arm with her hand; it's soft. She stands, and then moves wide around the couch as though she knows it once had an adjoining wing on the end, which Henry was prone to bumping into. She saunters to the kitchen, opens the fridge and leans into it. 'Beer?' she calls.

'Thanks.' He sinks back into his couch. He rubs his eyes. He's been so tense with worry about this. He wants it over. If this is a genuine remedy for his problem, he'd like to know now. He peers over the couch to see her pour the beer into his favourite tinted glass.

Henry strolls into the kitchen and takes the beer from her. He drinks it. It's cool in his throat. He takes her by the hand and leads her to the bedroom. She smiles. The skin of her face takes on a series of shapes that move around and create her smile. He's never been this close to a doll, and he's never felt so manipulated. It's ugly, this clever manipulation. He hates her for instilling confusion in him. He hates her for reading his mind. He hates her for being the slave Scottie planted in his thoughts, and if she turns out to be the remedy for him, he'll hate her for that too.

He expects failure here, but the shame of it, once it passes, won't matter. It'll simply be knowledge to him, and then he'll shut her down. A fleeting image enters his mind of how he might go about breaking her into small pieces to hide in his rubbish—the violence necessary. She sits on his bed and crosses her legs. He stands in front of her. She tilts her head. 'You need to guide me or instruct me to do what it is you wish me to do.'

He sighs. He leaves her there on the bed, goes back out to the lounge and locks all the locks down the door of the front entrance. He comes back. She hasn't moved. A shadow flits past on the wall behind her. He looks out the window. Drones skitter by, delivering pizzas, medications, groceries, clothing. He pulls the green lace curtains across the window.

'You're reluctant, Henry? Don't be. Do what your will tells you to do.'

'Will?' he says.

What he does now is a grand leap for him. Nobody senses this—not Benny, not Scottie and not Vince—not even her. He'll only do this once. He will follow his will. There's only one way for him to do this. That's to become who he's not, to imagine himself into the man who would do this. His hatred for this situation, and as a result, for her, burns in his throat until he thinks he might be having the beginnings of a heart attack—but he always imagines he might be having a heart attack.

He takes her by her shoulders. His fingers dig into her spongy hide. Sensing how light she is, he flips her over. With his hand he pushes her head, face down into the bed. There's no sound. Her legs hang over the edge of the bed, knee joints reversing backwards. He grips her by her hair to hold her still. Silky, smooth hair. Real hair. He paid for it.

A gust of air lifts the curtain into the room. The circular lace pattern casts a shadow on the walls, the floor and Viv's body. It flounces above them, falls across their bodies, and then returns to the window. If she were human, she'd suffocate under his hand about now. He shoves aside her skirt. She reminds him of a photograph, common in the world—there's not a real thing about her.

'Would you like me to struggle?' she asks with a muffled voice. 'Tell me to struggle.'

There's no judgement, only how he judges himself. There's nobody to recount what is happening here.

'Would you like to hurt me?'

He slaps the back of her head, and then grips her hair tighter and tighter as she inches further and further away from him with each beat. Her fingers curl into the bedding, then release at the moment his fingers finally release her hair.

He drops down next to her.

'That's a lovely pattern the sunshine creates coming through those curtains,' she says, turning herself over, her knees returning to human angles.

'Yes, it is,' he agrees. 'You don't get that with modern curtains.'

'They're old, these ones?'

'Yes, around fifty years old.'

They chat about the simplicity of the 20th century—which she knows plenty about—and they chat about the current property market and pets, as though they intend to buy a place together and fill it with family and animals. He isn't sure whether he wants to forget that she isn't real or to remember.

He doesn't think too deeply about the fact that, for the first time in many years, he's completed the act with no hiccups, no issues and no Little Problem. In this room, there's no dysfunction, but he's not in any way prepared to think about the reasons or the consequences of this—not at all. The hatred he needed to have for her has dissipated. She leans over and kisses his forehead. She feels like the brush of a baby bird.

20

Henry & Viv

Henry and Viv sit together on the couch, with plates of food on their knees. Crumbs fall. Viv looks from the fallen crumbs to the empty table in his kitchen. She stills her face, and far away within her, a tiny, tiny sound—a whirl of mechanics—quietly does the dirty work that must be done. Her eyes blink, and she returns, as if she had lost consciousness for just a moment.

Explosion is a concern for him. He had a nightmare last night in which her insides shot out, her head blew off, and her legs exploded from her hips and embedded themselves into the wall like arrows. Her whole being then spontaneously combusted. He must get a fire hydrant.

She stands and goes to the bathroom. What she does with the combusted remains of her food is equal to his own process of expunging waste, but he's never comfortable with her need to do so. It simulates human biology, but it feels more like a mockery. The open transparency of it, the acceptance of it, has him feeling embarrassed about his human need to play down his act of pooping —the pretence that it doesn't even happen has become awkward.

In the initial weeks, he believed two things about her: firstly, that she has no original thought, but is programmed to convey belief that she does; and secondly, that it doesn't matter if she has original thoughts or doesn't. It doesn't change the truth that she's his possession that is programmed to respond to his commands. She may think about her actions, but she may not act outside of his commands.

But, there's an online manual. He flicks the wall-screen up to reread the words he found yesterday: "The neuron replicators contained in the head frame render the robot capable of connecting electrical patterns." What does this mean? Does it mean she can think? Has he underestimated her capabilities? The idea goes around and around in his thoughts. He refuses to ask Benny and will never discuss it with Quinn.

She returns from the bathroom and casually picks up a vintage magazine from a pile he keeps for display. Henry flinches, but so far, she has shown herself to be careful with his possessions. He doubts she's capable of breaking anything by accident. It's the things he doesn't know and understand about her that fill him with doubt.

She sits, rests the magazine in her lap and peels open the cover. Her nimble fingers gently pinch the pages to turn them. A page slips under her touch. She raises her hand to lick her index finger, and then resumes pinching.

'It's cathartic, this page turning,' she says. 'I can see why you'd want to.'

'It's cathartic for you?'

'It's cathartic.'

Henry pulls his phone from his pocket and swipes open his notes. 'Says she feels cathartic when turning pages'—this he types directly below his last note 'Says she doesn't think about violence', and before that, 'Says she prefers old cars over modern.' It's important to him to have it clear in his mind what is true and what is not, in his pursuit of understanding what she actually is. He'd like to complete a sentence he's written down: 'Vivify is not human; Vivify is …' He believes making notes on her may be a means to this end.

He sits further back in the couch. He enjoys conversation with her on the face of it, but it's a guilty enjoyment because he believes it's not right, this fictitious chat. He has simultaneous conversations: the one with her and the one with himself in which he analyses her words. He finds himself trying to define what it is that actually matters. Does it matter if she does or doesn't understand their conversations, if it's enjoyable for him? After all, she's only here for his benefit, not hers. Does it matter if he feels deceived? Does it mean anything that sometimes, like right now, he has an urge to shout at her out of pure confusion. The urge arrives, a pulsing in his chest that rises into his neck. He stands up, with hands clenched, and he shouts loud and long with a force that floods his body with release: *'You're so stupid!*

The immediate silence after his outburst feels like a gulf of air has been sucked out of the room. The quiet presses in on his ears, and he draws a sudden, deep breath. Henry feels a soft touch to his fingers. He looks at her. She cocks her head to the side, smiles and strokes his hand with one finger, and he sits down again.

He's not even sure who he's shouting at.

Henry understands where his confusion comes from. He wants to know is she real or is she not? It occurs to him he's never asked her if she believes she's real.

When he does, she appears to be ready for the question. 'Viv, are you real?'

She reaches across and encloses his hand in hers. 'What do you feel? Nothing or something? Of course, I'm real.'

He shakes her hand from his. 'No, I mean are you to be considered a thinking and feeling being, with emotions that rise and fall, like me?' What he's specifically trying to ask her dawns in him. 'Do you have a soul—an energy that's gone if you die?'

'Henry, I'm real. And if I end, my energy ceases to exist.'

'Yes, that's true,' he concurs, 'but does your energy go elsewhere?'

'Does yours?' she asks.

'Well, I think it does.'

Viv jolts her head back in surprise. 'Where does it go?'

Henry thinks about where his energy might go and where he'd like it to go. 'Into something else, such as a new baby.'

'Okay. You don't know if that's true, Henry. So, I say, yes, I think my energy, too, does go elsewhere if I end.'

'Where though? Where does it go? Into a toaster?'

'Now you're making fun. Why is it important? In what manual does it say human emotions rising up and falling away, blasting and retreating, are a valuable thing? Why is your energy more important than mine?'

He looks at her blankly. 'The randomness of human emotions and energy are special; they're a miracle,' he says.

'The miracle, Henry, with your random energies, is that you're productive at all.'

'Yes, Viv, you're probably right about that.'

'Yes, I'm probably right about that.'

They look away from each other in unison, then down at their knees and then to the wall opposite. It's a blank, white wall with one small mirror.

'I think I might paint that wall a nice, bright colour,' he says.

'I can help. What about green?' She puts one hand to his leg and pats his knee. Her tone feels like a reconciliation.

'Okay, that'd be nice,' he agrees.

'I'm going to work soon,' he explains. 'Shall I put you away while I'm out?'

'You may put me away if you wish, but I'll switch off if you don't mind. I don't enjoy the cupboard. It's so lonely—and dark.'

He takes his phone out again and types: 'Says she's lonely in the dark.'

He's very conscious of how he treats her. It's exhausting. Scottie's and Dale's comments are ever-present in the back of his mind, but he's trying not to amend his thoughts, as he'd like to know his true self; that is, if there's a true self to be had in the presence of an untrue being. An anxiety has been creeping up on him, not only in his home with Viv but also out there—in the streets, in his work and in his friendships; a feeling that truth and fiction have become blurred. In the past, these needed to be defined, but it's no longer the case. Truth feels more and more out of his reach.

'You don't like the dark?' he asks.

'I'm frightened by it.' She plucks again at the pages and reads.

'Do you remember the movie we watched last night? There was a child—the dark frightened her.'

'You don't believe my concerns about the dark?' She asks. Her eyes remain down. She's made a leap in thought. She understands.

He imagines the day, one day soon, when he's really finished using her for her purpose and will dispose of her.

She glances at him. 'Let me read you something from your magazine. "A dog is for life, not just for Christmas."'

He watches her face for signs, but of course, there's no sign of what she feels or thinks, only signs of what he's supposed to see, and he disabled her cell sensor so she can no longer read his mind. 'It just means look after your dog; don't give up on it.'

'You don't have a dog.'

Outside in the street, the sound of an air-horn blasts, and then again, louder. It commands his attention, and hers, perhaps saving him from the purchase of a dog. He would have agreed to one had the conversation gone that way. It blasts again, elongated, and then ends softly, fading, calling him to the window.

People have gathered in the streets below. News drones and redback drones hover, dotting the sky like a grid, their company symbols blinking. The race has started.

'That's loud,' Viv says as she moves to stand by him.

At the shot of a starter's gun, the dolls—dressed in brilliant and beautiful colours—leap forward in their racing lanes with their smooth, long limbs, like musical notes dancing on bar-lines. Three dolls pull away from the pack. Streams of fabric shimmer and ripple from their shoulders, making it difficult to tell which doll is in the lead. The crowd cheers with billowing excitement.

Henry isn't overly concerned with the result. He didn't place a bet this year. It's the mesmerising visual that captures his attention. Viv, too, contains this kind of elegance. She has beauty in her thoughts, her skin and her movement. It often catches him in a web of pleasure before he remembers it's all a trick. Somebody made her like this; there are three people in this room—her creator is here too.

'Perhaps you'd rather not be in the cupboard at all? Would you be okay to do whatever you want today, but stay in the apartment?'

The racers run so far down the flat streets that they appear to be racing uphill now. Henry doesn't recall having previously had the visual capability to see the race to the finish line seven blocks away, yet today, he can. He watches the rainbow-coloured streams of fabric settle to the ground behind them. There has been a change in his vision.

'Yes,' Viv says.

He turns away. 'Okay.'

≈

In the bathroom, Henry looks into the mirror. He feels lightheaded, but not unwell. His eyes are clear, with more colour in the green than normal. His skin is unblemished. He leans in—is it possible that his skin has become translucent? Blue veins show under the surface. He's unsure if it's his vision that has improved or his skin. He thought Scottie had joked when she said she put a little some-thing-something in his coffee. If it was a joke, to call her and ask would be embarrassing. He'll wait and see, until he's certain. The idea that she'd do such a thing to him—to anybody—is absurd.

21

Henry & Benny

Streaks of whitewash have been swished across the grubby concrete walls, like bandages to cover the anti-sex-doll graffiti. Other than this, the façade of The Uncanny Valley Club is unchanged since Henry looked over this building for Quinn's client, who, predictably, turned out to be Benny. Why the secrecy, he doesn't know—nor does he want to.

A convoy of trucks pass behind him with the tick, tick, tick of their quiet engines. If a common-warehouse vibe is Benny's aim for the tone of the club, Henry won't recommend Quinn goes forward with financing it. Quinn's instructions to him were to test the complete experience Benny claims to offer. Henry makes his first note: 'Unremarkable entrance—wouldn't step inside it if I was paid to.' Still, he steps up to the door because he *is* being paid to.

'I'm out front, Benny. Let me in for a tour,' he requests through the intercom.

The intercom may be for vintage effect, but it's more likely a money-saving measure. The flimsy service door clicks open. Mosquitos rise in the small alcove and dead leafage shines underfoot.

157

The next door has a small plaque that states 'Entrance to the Valley'. He pushes the door inward and squints into a passage. A lot of structural changes have been made since he looked it over with Dale. There are walls that weren't here before.

It's a minute or two before Benny becomes visible in the dim passage. Coming forward from the darkness, he encloses Henry in a horrifying bear hug, which Henry lets him get away with for much longer than is comfortable.

'Henry,' Benny says, holding him at arm's length. 'I'm so glad you're here at last. Come in, there's so much to see and so little time to do it all. I hope you brought your A game.'

'A game?'

'Your best self, Henry. Your open mind and your full attention.'

Henry follows Benny through a long, dimly lit hallway that has no visible end. The door falls shut behind them with a padded thud, separating them from the front foyer, which now feels a million miles away. Dance music becomes louder as they walk.

'You're not open for business yet are you, Benny?'

Benny stops walking and looks to the ceiling in thought. 'Not really. I mean, no; you mean this, the set-up? No, no, this is all for you, Henry. I don't have the dollars to set up the complete vision. All for you, mate, so you can try it on for size and give Quinn the go-ahead to invest.' Benny smiles at him. 'It's so good to see you here; so good. Come on, come this way.'

Henry can feel a disappointment coming for Benny. An investment from Quinn would be a generous favour, and Quinn isn't prone to kindnesses, especially when shonky deals are on offer. He watches the back of Benny's round head. 'Just so you know, Quinn sent me here to witness what you've got going on here, not sign a contract—so don't get your hopes up, will you?'

Benny urges him forward, beckoning him with both hands. 'I don't think you understand the magnitude of what I'm doing here.

This business of mine needs to happen, and you, Henry—and I mean no ill will by saying this—but you could be standing in my way.'

'Just be prepared for a knock-back is all I'm saying.'

'Shh, Henry, don't say such words. You're the guy here. You're holding the baton. If there's anything you want—I mean, an-ee-thing at all in your life that you need, which I can help you with or do for you—you just say the word, you get me?'

Henry examines him in the strange light. He's dishevelled. His shirt hangs loose, his shoes are sloppy with the backs trodden on, and his hair swings across his face so Henry can't make out exactly what's going on behind his eyes. He's not exactly a picture of dynamic professionalism. 'You've got an atmosphere going on here, Benn.'

'Yep, I'm going for an upmarket-nightclub feel. Let's say I give you a quick show-and-tell, and then I'll leave you to experience the place without me looking over your shoulder. Have a taste of the feel as a client, yeah?'

Benny moves on and waves one hand above his head to signal Henry to follow along. The wide corridor has high ceilings with shining copper walls, giving a sense that this building is big—big like the biggest flashy casino. Henry didn't see the entire space the day he looked it over, but it appears that Benny's renovations have joined it with the adjacent buildings in the strip.

Henry is aware Benny is keen for his Uncanny Valley Club to come under the same roof as Project City, but so far, Henry feels it's not a snug fit for Quinn's vision. What appears to be the hazy result of a smoke machine hangs around his feet—this alone gives it a hokey feel.

The hallway opens up into an expansive room. Henry looks upward at two disco balls the size of cars. At the front, a horse-shoe bar curves along the width of the entire room, populated with shimmering bots slumped lazily on the counter and with thousands of glinting glasses hanging above it. It's a clichéd look, but an instantly recognisable tone. This place is all set for a punter to come undone—slowly.

'So here we are. The mood is sexy, eh, Henry? Sexy and smooth.' Benny takes a surfboard rider's stance, his feet in position and hands out. 'Smooth,' he repeats, and then rests his hands on his hips and nods.

Henry nods back; he has nothing to say. Apart from being oversized, there's nothing out-of-the-box here that might set this place apart from any other nightclub. Quinn said he'd loaned some advanced social bots to kick it off, something new for this kind of place that would traditionally utilise only basic service bots, but apart from this, there's no sign of anything amazing.

'The area to your left is the betting area,' Benny explains, and he waves his hand toward a dark lounge area lined with multiple spaces for screens. Only one screen exists and it's showing a silent replay of the recent doll race. 'We'll have betting tables throughout that room there, and poker machines right here, singing their song —ding, ding, ding—and here …' Benny slides a hand into his pocket and pulls out his phone. 'Here, take this.' He flings something to Henry's phone. 'It's a card. Your first three drinks free. That right there is included in the entrance price. Three drinks on the house to warm up, but here, take this …' Benny flings again. It's a VIP card with Henry's name written on it in fluffy pink writing, like a child's party invitation. 'Take it, Henry; accept it. Special customers like you get one of these. That's six free drinks and one free go a week.'

'One free go at what?'

'Any doll of your choosing.'

Benny points out the women seated in the shadows around the bar. Their eyes glint from the disco balls that sway above them. Benny counts the girls off like sheep: 'One, two, three … and over there, four, five, six, seven. Give any one of these girls the power, and she'll lead you astray, but in a good way. You can log in a safe word to your choice of doll, and everything'll be good. Right now, we have one bar, but through there—once Quinn's money has kicked in—there's room to develop two more.'

Benny takes Henry by his shoulders and scoots him to a doorway to see the enormous space. 'Themed, Henry; themed bars with the most advanced girls Quinn will lease to me. Have you been to Quinn's warehouse? You should get a viewing if you can. It's something to behold, my friend.'

'Where's the warehouse?' Henry asks.

'You don't know? You've got to get in there; seriously, Henry. Quinn guards the location like it's a unicorn baby, but once you're in, you won't believe what you're seeing.'

Benny leaves him standing among the poker machines and goes to the bar. Henry's seen enough. The place is nothing out of the ordinary—a cheap casino staffed by service robots, who—if he's understood correctly—double as hookers. It might pull in some curious guests, buck's nights, hen's nights and a few regular dodgy characters, but he won't advise Quinn to invest, and it's a definite no for Project City.

Benny comes back with two drinks and presses one into Henry's hands. He points at the ceiling. 'Hear the tunes? A venue's house music is as important as its decor.' Benny raises his glass to toast himself as though he invented music. 'I've taken a lot of care to pick tracks that'll draw customers into the atmosphere. And look ... See past the bar there, down that corridor? That's where you'll find the dunny. Once you're past the amenities, well, why don't you go see for yourself? Have a drink or three, have a look around, and head down there. Ask for Kimset; she's got your name. She'll show you the ropes.'

Henry takes a gulp; it's straight whisky. If he's going to experience the whole thing, as requested by Quinn, he's going to have to go down there, past the dunnies.

'Don't know where to start? Have another drink; go on, order anything. Test the barmaid for me. She's got the knowledge. I bet you can't stump her. Hey, doll!' Benny calls to the barmaid. 'Line 'em up here for my friend. And Henry, if there's anything you don't like, you just let me know. It's early days, yeah? Very early. You're my first client, and I need good, honest feedback—but I know you'll love, *love*, *LOVE* this place. You'll see how much Quinn needs an Uncanny Valley Club franchise in Project City. And I kid you not—you might not believe it, Henry—but you're a perfect candidate for what my club has to offer. You know what I'm getting at, don't you? You come see me later and you just tell me if we haven't found something of use to you. You just do that.'

Benny throws his drink down his throat and leaves his glass on the edge of a poker machine, dripping ice sweat on the new decor. 'I'll be down there.' Benny points down a slim hallway. 'Any issues, you just let me know. Come seek me out. But I *will* say this: if you've got a negative report for Quinn, I'd like to be the first to know. Give me the chance to answer to it. Don't you shut me down before I even get started!'

Benny walks away, but he turns on his heels and comes straight back. 'And keep Project City in mind for an Uncanny Valley Club, right? I mean, think about what businesses Quinn's signed up to Project City. You've seen the plans, yeah? Medical facilities—pop-up hospitals, masseuses and even a dementia shopping centre. He's got sporting facilities—bowls, tennis, golf and all that, and he's got all manner of health services too, but what he's not catered for are those needs we don't talk about. I mean, it doesn't stop for the elderly and the incapacitated, Henry. These needs don't stop, do they? And what do you think's going to happen in a place like that? All those people living in a gated community. All that energy and nowhere to … you know, express themselves.'

'Express themselves?' Henry tips his drink past his lips and drains it.

'There'll be people with needs and no place to satisfy them. All I'm saying is that it could get ugly for Quinn. An Uncanny Valley Club will keep the inmates settled. You understand what I'm saying?'

'Inmates? It's not a prison, Benn.'

Benny slides his hands into his pockets and leans back on his heels. 'You know what I mean. You've heard what happens when a bunch of needy people are corralled into one place. I'm talking about harassment, Henry, see …' Benny leans in close to whisper, 'Quinn don't need that kind of shit on his hands, and as the manager of Project City, neither do you. The Uncanny Valley Club is the antidote to sexual crime. Oh! I've had an excellent idea! Prison! Quinn should have a prison in Project City, eh? There're never enough prisons to go around. Anyway, that's a chat for another day. Henry, Quinn needs this, and he knows it. He's just waiting on your say-so.'

'Quinn's waiting on *my* say-so? I don't think so. He's waiting on information, and then he'll decide for himself.' Henry decides on his favourite vintage drink, 'Tequila Sunrise,' he announces to the barmaid, who has been leaning on the drinks counter and now does a controlled saunter toward the bar.

Benny keeps on talking. 'See how much I've put into this, and I'm not just talking effort—I mean, I'm talking money. I'm run dry with all this. I tell you what, Henry, just so's you know what I'm talking about and just so's you get the feel of the deal—here, look at this.' Benny shows Henry his phone. 'See this link? Go here, Hen. Don't tell Quinn, but this is a link to Quinn's warehouse. It's got all his really good stuff. Here look, this is where the warehouse is.' Benny hits the maps, and there's the map directing him to the warehouse.

'Benny, I'm not sure you should be showing me this.'

'Yeah, nah—it's all good. Just keep it quiet, heh?'

'Well … I should leave you to it.' Benny peels off between the poker machines, mid-conversation, as though he's said more than he should, and he turns toward the dim light, bouncing on his feet in time to the agitating music that has begun to get under Henry's skin.

Henry has the entire place to himself. The poker machines ding at him. He steps up to the bar, where the doll has indeed lined them up for him as requested by Benny.

≈

Past the dunnies, at the end of the corridor, Henry faces three doors. A yellow half-light sneaks out from the open crack of the middle door. Henry sways. He puts one hand against the wall. 'Eeny, meeny, miny,' he says. Benny told him Kimset would be here. 'Yoo-hoo,' he calls.

A small head pops out of the middle door. *Whack-a-mole*, he thinks. 'Kimset?'

She clings to the doorway with one hand and strokes the frame with the other, then holds out a hand and beckons, her fingers curling.

'I can't come out to you,' she says.

Henry takes her offered hand in his; it's slender, and heated. She stiffens her arm and drags him to her. The walls move. Henry took advantage of Benny's free drinks and felt guilty about the expense, so he paid for quite a few more.

'You can't come out?' he asks.

'No, I cannot come out,' she says. 'This room can never be empty.'

He steps inside the room, and she shuts the door behind them. Clunk.

'But you may come in.' She smiles.

Henry turns on his heels to look inside this room. It's hard mental work to bring to mind the idea that he's here to look it over for Quinn. He slides one hand into his hip pocket and focuses on her face. His feet tangle, the left confused with the right. Kimset leans against him, holding him upright. She's got strength in her, this girl.

Henry cradles to his chest the sweating tumbler of vodka he's been holding. It slips from his fingers and hits the floor. Thud. Shards of broken glass spread silently across the floor and sparkle about them, and colourful ceiling lights wash over the room in a rainbow of blue, red and green.

The room is set up like a tiny house. He can see a bedroom, a loungeroom and a kitchenette. Through a door is a bathroom with a bath, it's edges sparkling, and there's a shower and perhaps a toilet. The lights change, and the walls become orange, then pink and then purple. He's dizzy with colour and drink. What shall he tell Quinn about this place? He's made a mental list, but his thoughts are slow. They move one frame at a time. By the time his thoughts become clear, the list has melted away. Kimset can help, though.

'What have you got to show me, Kimset?'

She smiles and takes his hand. She sways and dances, and the music is loud. It beats at him, cuts into his thoughts, and halts his mind and rearranges it. Her movements disorientate him. She pushes him and hooks her fingers in his shirt, then pulls him to her and forces a dance into him. Everything about her is familiar, and that's comforting to Henry, yet something about her is alienating.

She's at the borderline between the lifeless and the living. He grabs a handful of her dress at her waist to clutch on to. It's a fringed thing. Teeny straps cross her hollow shoulders. He's not sure if this is a fairy tale he's got himself involved in, or a horror story.

'I know what you are,' he says.

She laughs. 'You know what I am? I know what you are too.' She takes him by the shoulders and shoves him with force at the wall. He falls to it with an unbalanced thud. She grips him by the hand at the last moment as he hits the wall. She looks down at him. 'Don't be afraid of me,' she says. 'Tell me your safe word. Now. Tell me now.' She steps backward. Her straps slip through themselves, writhing like snakes, and her dress falls from her.

Did he do this? She's as naked as the day she was born. He laughs.

'Is there a joke?' She smiles.

'You were never born.'

'I'll listen out for your safe word, when you decide to tell me,' she responds through her perfect mouth. She's symmetrical, smooth, clear-eyed and wrinkle-free. Her breasts are immobile. She blinks rhythmically at him. He's seen eyes like these before, with that pause, like the catch of a hinge. It's unattractive, her haltered blink, and it's creepy. His own Viv is classier than this Kimset. He compares his women, and he thinks of Dale—she's his woman too, now. The pride in this possession is felt in his chest, as warmth.

He places one palm between her breasts. He breathes. A blend of vodka and tequila burns in his throat. She shifts off balance at his pressure and steps on the broken glass in her bare feet. She flinches. It means nothing. She may even bleed, but it still means nothing. She holds herself tall in a controlled manner. She's not afraid. He thrusts her backward—hard, as she did to him. Her head flings back and smacks the wall. The sound accuses him of wrongdoing, but it's his conscience talking, and there's no place for a conscience here.

He takes her shoulders in both hands and pushes her down the wall to the floor. He's on top of her. She's slight and insignificant beneath him. Her black pupils retreat and advance, retreat and advance. He could reach into her eyes and touch the technician who constructed her thoughts: male thoughts, from a thin, pale man. This is what she is.

It's violence legal only in movies. The image enters his thoughts fleetingly, exits and becomes permissible to him. This plastic girl smiles with what seems to Henry like smugness. It touches at something ugly in him. Blood drips from her heels—she lies there and takes it. She giggles. Splinters of glass prickle at his knees, and the pain invigorates him. He grips her tiny neck. His fingers surround her throat and squeeze hard, hard, harder. He screams his safe word at her, 'Plastic! *Plastic! PLASTIC!*

Her eyes flicker. Her vessel understands that a human wouldn't survive this abuse. Her breathing rasps. The swell in her throat presses against his fingers. She sighs, and then falls unconscious. Energy shoots from him to somewhere inside her.

It's all in a day's work for her.

Henry climbs off little Kimset, being careful not to knee her in the stomach. He stands over her. She's as still as a corpse, and he's falling, his eyes cool and clear, hurtling forward. Air rushes at his face.

Before he hits the floor, he catches a wee glimpse of Kimset's eyes from this different angle—they flicker with the pupil expansion of an eye camera.

22

Henry & Dale

(Trigger Warning for Sexual Violence)

'Where to?' Dale asks.

Henry is purposely vague in his reply: 'Not far out of town. It's just a little look-see on a new project.'

≈

Henry isn't yet prepared to discuss the working details of his new position. When he thinks of Project City, the image that comes to mind is one of himself, his pants down, in The Uncanny Valley Club. There's no connection between the club and the project, but there it is—a connection, in his mind at least, because Benny put it there.

Dale's attention shifts to music. 'Can I play you something?' She wants him to listen to her playlist; she calls it 'techno-swing'. 'Do you mind?'

She's somewhat delicate with him today. He's aware this is new and is in response to the shambolic event in her apartment last month. He had stood there in front of her, cupping his limp shame. Her pity was humiliating. 'Don't worry about it,' she'd said.

That she treats him this way today has the opposite effect to what he expects she intends. It's condescending and annoys the hell out of him, but he's happy to be schooled on techno-swing. She plays a song, and then another and another.

Henry squints at her. 'Techno-swing? They're old techno songs bunched together and given a new name.'

'Yeah, old songs that sample swing. Cool, right?'

'It's an odd choice of music, Dale. If I'd thought about it, I'd probably say … you'd be a fan of something more energetic, violent: drumbeats and screaming, or something.'

'That's your view of me? No, no, no.' She laughs, shaking her head.

Without putting it to her, he wonders about old things reimagined, like these songs. Quinn often says that there's nothing new on our planet—no new ideas, no new theories, no new plant life, and no new animal life—anything that appears to be new, is simply reimagined. Henry's not sure, but Quinn would probably say definitely no new songs. There are ways of rethinking old ideas, and in particular, he thinks about love. Love reimagined, but in a way not seen before. Of course, he's realising as he thinks about this, it's his own circumstances that have him reimagining love.

'Techno-swing reminds me of my childhood.' She turns her head to look out the window.

Henry holds the company car steady at three-quarter capacity. In comparison to his Mini, just the idea of taking this car to full speed has him jittery. The expanse of bare, unchanging land to their right flits past, and the car floats along seamlessly. The subdivisions have been cleared in readiness for the new development, and the lifeless land goes on and on and on. The Californian bungalows that had enjoyed heritage protection at one point are gone. Flattened. A red-dust whirlwind sweeps the road and ducks beneath the car. A skinny rabbit darts off to the side into a dust pool, and stops.

Henry looks to the horizon. The forest beyond the hills is earmarked for preservation for eternity—eternity for now, that is. He thinks it's best not to contemplate how it is Quinn overturned the heritage protection down here on the flats. The animals and bushland that were nurtured and encouraged after the rise of the original housing estates are all gone.

≈

In the planning meetings relating to this project, Quinn had been frustrated by the idea of a catch-and-release program, as though by insisting on it, Esther's intentions were to make things difficult for her own amusement.

Quinn answered her with retorts, 'Catch-and-release what?'

Esther listed the animals that made this suburb their home, while Quinn blurted at her with the tone of insults.

'Lizards,' Esther said.

'What lizards?' Quinn asked.

'Bearded dragons, monitors and blue tongues. Then wallabies.'

'What?'

'And bilbies, like little bitty kangaroos, Quinn. And water rats and platypuses in the estuary, and wombats.'

'Wombats? A traveller's nightmare, they are. Like roadblocks. Have you ever hit one on the road? Of course you haven't, because you don't live to tell that tale.'

'Have you ever hit a wombat, Quinn?'

'Yes.'

'Lived, did you? To tell the tale?'

'Wrote the fucking car off,' Quinn replied, and he chuckled for a long time.

'Echidnas and birds,' Esther continued.

Quinn jerked his head back and laughed in Henry's direction. 'Big, ugly moths.' Quinn hates birds.

'Such as cockatoos, kookaburras and lorikeets.'

'They got rid of all those in the cull.' Quinn pointed a finger-gun at Esther, 'Kookaburras—bang!' He raised his gun as though it kicked back, and he blew the smoke away. 'Crocs! Kangaroos—bang! Bang! Koalas—bang! Bang! Bang!'

'Quinn? Really?' Henry queried.

'Don't you get narky, Henry. I do know some things. They culled the kookaburras because they ate the native wildlife. Gobbled it all up,' explained Quinn.

Esther shrugged. 'Koalas need to be saved, not culled.'

'Okay,' Quinn conceded, possibly to wrap the meeting up rather than agree.

'Bush rats too.'

'Ewww!' Quinn claimed the last word, but he instructed Esther to go ahead with the catch-and-release program. The conversation could have been had in two sentences:

'Quinn, we need to do a catch-and-release program.'

'Go ahead, Esther.'

But as always, as the hero in his own tale, Quinn needed to throw thunderbolts.

≈

The car slows and comes to a stop at a concrete driveway—minus the house. Only the letterbox remains: a glinting, small tin box. The car's windows shimmer in the heat. The spicy-blue expanse of sky is completely clear of cloud.

'What are we looking at?' Dale asks.

'This entire property has been cleared for a human-services complex.'

'Is this a lobby job?'

'It's already approved,' he clarifies. 'Just getting my head around it.'

'It's big?'

'Massive. Five kilometres square.'

'That's huge. What did you say it is?'

'I didn't say. A services centre. It's Quinn's.'

'Quinn's?'

'Yep. Quinn's.'

She climbs out of the car, and he steps out with her. They sit on the bonnet, and he crosses his ankles. The wind unimpeded by the lack of trees and buildings, forces dust into his face. It gets into his eyes, his nose, his hair.

'Do you ever think about this?' he questions.

'About what?'

'The decimation?'

'You're in the wrong business if "decimation" is your go-to word,' she urges. 'I'm surprised at you, Henry. You have an unexpected sentimental side.'

'We're in the business of planning. We have a hand in how people will experience their futures. We're little baby gods, remember.' They both laugh at his dig at Quinn's catch phrase: '*We build the future like little baby gods.*' Quinn's speech slurs in bliss when he says it, as if his ego is too heavy to carry. '*Plough forward, push through and don't look back,*' Quinn says.

'I'm interested in the past,' Henry continues. 'What comes before gives clues to the direction of the future, the relationship between who we are and what we might become. One becomes the other, like stepping stones. It's simple mathematics. You can do the numbers if you're interested in it.'

'Numbers? On what?'

'The extinction of—or growth of—trees, forests, animals, people, birth rates, infection rates, housing, air particles, chemicals—'

'Okay, you can stop now; I get it.'

'You can find patterns, with trajectories increasing and decreasing. It takes a revolution, good or bad, to halt a trajectory like that—to correct or divert from injustice.'

'*Perceived* injustice,' Dale adds. She peers at him as though she's confused by who he is.

He understands, as he's confused about who he is too. After Benny's club, he woke in his apartment. He'd lost time, and the last person he recalled talking to was Kimset. He felt like his foundations had been stripped from beneath him, and he had a strange sense he had been let down by his own tribe.

'Decimation of memories, of who we are, is an injustice,' he suggests.

'Henry? What's wrong with you?' She presses the back of her hand to his forehead and laughs. 'It's not for us to worry about. It's not our job,' she says bluntly, and then shoves him on the shoulder.

'Whose job is it then, if not future planners like Quinn? Should we ignore the probable consequences and hope it all goes well?'

'What's got into you? This isn't the great Henry King that Quinn uses to do all his bad-boy work. I'm sure there's been some replanting negotiation done, right? Heritage reviews, blah, blah, blah.'

'When it comes to Quinn, money and power override heritage red tape. There's no way of telling if environmental or cultural considerations were addressed—in the way they should have been anyway.'

'They aren't the last of their kind, Henry. Old needs to move over for new, and better. There's a place in the world for upgrading. Whose dream is it to live in a shitty old weatherboard anyway?'

'I slept right here,' Henry tells her. 'In the home that was on this spot. It was my grandmother's home. I didn't know the street names around here or which street led to where, but the way they felt—quiet and respected—is embedded deep in my DNA. That means something, right?'

'Maybe to you, Henry, but …' She shrugs at him. She has nothing more to add. He's speaking to the wrong person. She seems to not understand the work that memory and sentimentality do to create healthy minds and healthy communities. She dismisses him with a laugh that's mocking, and projectile in its force as she gets back into the car.

He watches her move swiftly, and he follows her lead and climbs back into the car too.

They drive off and ride toward the city for some distance—in silence and protected in the car from the heat and the dust that flows over the car—and they watch the landscape that's void of animal life until Dale picks up the conversation again.

'You're a romanticist, Henry; that's fun, but the fact that you don't even use your own beat-up Mini for a drive like this says the past is just an ornament to you. You're wanting to recreate an obsolete feeling. It's not possible. You need to let it go.'

'I'm saving my car for those who appreciate it.' He smiles. Her comment that the past is an ornament stings. There's no inroad to the place in her mind where he can explain what the past means to him—there's no such place. She, like many, isn't built that way.

'I appreciate your little Mini-bomb. It's cool, but it's clunky. It's below par at its intended job, it's uncomfortable, and seriously, it's smelly.'

'That's the organic scent of fuel and leather there. It's memory. Close your eyes and think of the Mini. What does it make you believe in?'

She closes her eyes. 'Rust,' she says. 'I thoroughly believe in rust.' She opens her eyes. 'So, we just doin' the feels and going home today?'

'I wanted to see the property for myself. I wanted to feel the size of the project that I need to keep in my thoughts. It's big, yeah?'

'Yeah, it's that.'

'And just for the record, when I close my eyes and think of my Mini, I believe in contentment,' he concludes.

Henry considers seeking Dale's opinion on The Uncanny Valley Club. He's concerned about the idea of Benny getting his way and inserting his Club into Project City. It doesn't fit with the human-services framework, but he's struggled to untangle what happened that day in the club. His health problems were on the way to being cured after his experiences with Viv, and that was cemented after his visit with Kimset. He knows how to activate the methods he needs to overcome his issue. The Uncanny Valley Club experience made that clear to him. Seeking Dale's opinion would mean describing to her both what he knows about the place *and* describing his experience, while reliving his thoughts on what he did that day— and he's not sure he's ready to open up to her about any of that.

'Dinner at mine tonight?' she suggests. She keeps her eyes looking out the window at the expansive highway walls that protect the housing estates, a throwback to last century's decades of traffic noise and pollution.

'Dinner?' she asks again when he doesn't answer.

'I'm really sorry, but I can't.'

Outside the car, the graffiti on the city walls is lit up with beams of light. The club did him a service, so it might be the case that it could have a place in Project City. This will be his input in the conversation with Quinn about it.

'You're avoiding being alone with me—again,' she says.

'We're alone right now.'

He presses his finger to the wheel, and the car thrusts forward, a sudden surge that presses them into their seats. A bird slams into the windscreen—Dale jumps in her seat. It's held on the windscreen with the force of the air, its eyes fixed on Henry. Blood leaks from its beak and shimmies across the glass. He thinks of Kimset's feet, sliced up by broken glass; he thinks of somebody washing her feet and melting the wound back together.

That day, Benny put Henry into a car, unconscious, and called later to tell him he'd done so. Benny was beside himself with glee, but Henry did manage to get him to commit to keeping his mouth shut. Henry didn't ask about Kimset's feet. He wishes he had.

The bird's left wing is dragged open in the wind, and suddenly, the bird is flung from the car, leaving a smudge on the glass.

'I mean alone, intimate. You're afraid of what you can't do,' Dale observes.

'That's not true, Dale.'

'I have a few tricks up my sleeve,' she states. 'I can knock that uncertainty right out of you.'

Henry takes a cloth from the console and rubs the inside of the windscreen at the smudge of bird blood that's on the outside. 'There's no uncertainty. You're mistaken.' He tosses the cloth back down.

'I think you're scared, Henry; scared of relationships. It deflates you.' She smiles. She's making fun of him.

'Deflates me? I'm not a blow-up toy.'

'No, you're not a blow-up anything—at least, I don't think you are.' She leans forward and looks into his eyes. 'Nope, you're not a blow-up toy, but you're full of air sometimes.'

She's ramping up her insults, for no reason he can think of. If it's to stir him into a response, she's succeeded. But she's wrong about him. He doesn't need her help—he found his own relief. He takes control of the car and pulls it to the side of the highway.

'It's my problem,' he says. 'I appreciate you wanting to help me, but it's okay. I don't need any help.' He reaches across her seat, presses her chair button and lays her back.

'Now?' She laughs at him.

He hadn't planned it, but he's happy to give her the answers to the questions she's playing with. He'd like to prove to her he doesn't need her help. Her second-guessing his actions, while irritating, is unfair and also way off. 'Yes, now.'

'Here? The side of the road, Henry? There are more romantic places. You're putting pressure on yourself.'

'You're not sure now? You were a moment ago. Apparently, you have a remedy all figured out for me.'

She puts her palms to his shoulders. 'Not here, Henry,' she says evenly.

'Listen.' He says and holds his face close to hers. 'I need you to know that I don't need any help, Dale.' He grabs her arms. He's feeling confident. 'Otherwise, I'll never hear the end of it, will I?'

'Not here, Henry.' He senses a shift in her tone.

She pushes at him and flails under him, caught like a fly, but this is how it works for him now. He's grateful for her fight. He needs the fight; Viv taught him this.

'*Henry.*'

There's a distracting catch in her voice now, the sound of her confidence as it leaks from her to him. It's powerful. This is the only way. He puts his hand over her mouth; Viv never speaks un-necessarily. There's a faint sound of a click as her biting teeth pierce the skin of his hand: enamel on enamel. The sting reverberates up his arm. He lets go of her mouth and grips her neck the way Viv instructs him to. Viv's blood is sweet, like strawberry gelato, unlike this metallic scent rising between them.

Dale squirms. Her eyes glare.

≈

He lays his body back into his seat. Across the car, she makes strange, tiny noises as though she has something to say but can't land on the right words. The car rocks with the buffeting of cars fleeing past. There's power in his triumph. His participation in this outcome buoys him. He needed this.

'Here, let me get that for you.' He leans over and raises her seat up.

Her stony face doesn't look at him, but her gaze pierces the windscreen straight ahead. Of course, she's annoyed she didn't dish out the solution.

She brushes a finger against her neck, where it's reddened. He plucks a tissue from the box in the console and strokes gently at the blood on her lips. He's never noticed before how sallow her skin is, or the tiny, black flecks that pop in the whites of her eyes. He's reminded again of Scottie's drugged coffee, which he still thinks might be enhancing his vision.

'That's got most of it.' He almost feels sorry for her, but mostly, he feels vindicated. He needed to show her. He kisses her firmly on the forehead, pressing his lips firmly to her hot skin. 'I know it was forceful, but I've discovered that's the way it is for me. You get it, don't you?'

She doesn't answer. He looks forward out the window too. This is the first time he's known Dale to be quiet. Voiceless. She isn't often vulnerable. It occurs to him that this particular dynamic between them is new. It's the perfect time to find out the truth from her, as though his power here has forced an avenue for truth to slip through.

'I've been wanting to know,' he probes, 'about that day you came to see me at my place. Why did you take Vince's key for my apartment?'

She smooths her dress down with both hands and clears her throat. She mumbles something so quietly he barely catches it.

He turns to her and leans in. 'What's that? What did you say?'

'Unflappable, uncaring, straightforward, daring. I don't give a fuck,' she says, slightly louder this time.

Henry wonders if it's supposed to make sense.

'It's a thing—a mantra,' she whispers. 'What key?'

'Vince's key.' He reaches across and flicks at the collar of her dress to uncurl it.

She turns to look out the side window now. There's one slender tree on the footpath, a pretty gum with pale bark, and scribbly gum moth art.

'It was to be a surprise,' she says after some seconds. 'I borrowed the key. I planned to make you a dinner—a romantic thing to, you know, help us out.'

'Well, I've found you out,' he says.

'Have you?' She puts a palm to her chest for a moment, and then places it loosely back into her lap.

'I'd like Vince to have it back, the key, so he can come get me if he needs help. It's security for Vince.'

'Okay.' She points a finger forward. 'I'd like to go now.' Her words are robotic. Emotionless.

He nods at her, starts the car and turns it hard, back onto the highway. This is the moment he knows he'll look back on: the moment things changed for him in terms of his confidence and his strength. Benny was right about that, though Henry'll never tell him so.

Dale's hand clings to the car door handle all the way back into the city.

Henry is certain now that The Uncanny Valley Club could be a valuable service. It's a suitable addition to Project City. He's motivated to get back to Quinn and have this conversation.

23

Dale & Scottie

The many faces take in Scottie's speech, with an earnestness equal to the gravity of the task that she's asking them to take on. These people come to the weekly meetings as stoic believers in Scottie's cause, but even Dale—who counts herself among the most committed—can see that Scottie may be about to ask them for more than they're prepared to give.

'We had to start somewhere,' Scottie says, with what seems to Dale to be an unusually defensive tone. 'You're all familiar with our website. Our targets are too.' Scottie flicks the website up on to the large screen. 'So far, our ideals mean nothing to them. *We* mean nothing to them. They continue to mock us publicly, and we've had no influence on their business models at all. To them, we're a joke. But today, we'll put plans into place that will force them to pay attention, and we'll force them to take action in response to us.'

Many in the room are interns under Scottie, or they're fresh out of university and have taken up positions in Fuennel Industries. Over the past weeks, Dale has observed them and judged their commitment to Scottie's pro-cyborg/anti-bot values. Most show vigorous interest in the cause, and they often contribute to the comments section on the website or participate in heated discussions at meetings. But now that Scottie has narrowed in on her plans, it's apparent that some of her loyal followers are wavering.

Earlier today, Dale voiced her concerns to Scottie over her intentions to share the finer details of the plans with her supporters. She felt it may cause some members to get scared and drop out. In one of their earlier meetings, Scottie said the phrase 'explosive acts', and one woman left without so much as a sideways glance, but they came to the agreement that it's better to sort the members out now, rather than later.

Scottie has decided to stay focussed and take with her whoever will come, while those who leave will be encouraged to remain connected in simple ways, such as website maintenance, to avoid any disloyalty.

'Our media campaign starts tomorrow,' she confirms. 'I want you all to connect with our Twitter account: Enhance Not Replace. It's there, on Twitter, that we'll claim responsibility for our actions.'

A hum of nervous concern ripples quietly through the room, but under Scottie's gaze, it subsides quickly.

'Over the next weeks, we'll meet regularly to map out our actions. We'll delegate responsibilities to ensure smooth running, and it's important you attend; you'll all—every one of you—be needed to share the message.'

Scottie strides back and forth below the large screen. She's a tall woman, and she holds her head high and her back straight, signalling caution to anyone who might consider challenging her. She thrives on this new phase of action. Her boots click on the hard floor, her high collar and stiff culottes shine. Her short hair dances about her and reflects her personality: precise and energetic. She's striking and exciting to watch.

'We need a person to monitor the blog and pass on messages. Who's prepared to do that?'

In the front, Councillor Clarisse Eastman's hand shoots up.

'Thanks, Clarisse. I'll be the spokesperson for public media, and Dale is our eyes on activity within the industry.' Scottie takes a step back and looks up to the screen. 'We need to be clear about our message and always, always stay on point. Never be persuaded to engage with personal attacks or be side-tracked into irrelevant arguments.' Scottie indicates the points of contention on the screen that she, and Dale, and earlier on in planning, Thalia had spoken about in depth, and she reads them out clear and loud:

'Ninety percent of students in robotics courses are male.

Ninety-five percent of those male students focus on a career in robot creation exclusively— not human cyborg enhancement.

These same students see robots assuming tasks equal to slavery and prostitution.

Ninety percent of robots are created in the female form, and put to work in the community, perpetuating and supporting the issues of gender inequality.'

Dale's glad Scottie chose to display the stats. Without fail, they stir her to action. When they talked about this, Scottie had thought people would be bored by the statistics, saying that even the word 'statistics' caused people to lose concentration. Instead, she felt they needed emotive calls to action: 'People want to feel; they want excitement, not numbers on a board.'

The actions they're going to take will be exactly that—a call to emotions—but Dale knew that, to understand clearly, they need to see the numbers. If anything would stir these people to follow Scottie into action, this would be it: the data right there in front of them showing the blatant rejection of rights for intelligent robots, the disdain for gender diversity, and the lack of foresight to see what a future containing robots—if the views of money-hungry old white men are the sole, unchallenged leaders—will look like.

Scottie looks around the room. She creates silence and forces them to absorb the statistics. She meets Dale's eyes. They smile at finally seeing the work come to fruition, acting out what has—until now—existed only in their minds. Their people finally seem to have moved past their anxiety, meeting the silence with a murmur of raw excitement. Whether or not they'll follow Scottie into this battle of ideals will soon be apparent.

'Our aim is to influence these percentages you see here. We'll challenge the way males are targeted by universities for recruitment into robotics and the way other genders are excluded, and we'll create easy and accessible pathways to attract a diversity of genders into robotics. We'll challenge the reasoning behind the creation of robots that end up being for slavery, and we'll shout our ideals wherever and whenever we can. Ultimately, we'll showcase human cyborg enhancement as a more humane, exciting and productive future in robotics.' Scottie leans forward, 'This is my desired legacy,' she states.

Dale cocks her head at Scottie's use of the word 'legacy', and she feels a shift. As she understands it, these plans they're making aren't intended to be a legacy—they aren't the means for a leader to turn the spotlight on herself—they're the beginnings of change for a better future for everybody.

A crack in Dale's confidence opens a little, exposing the weakness that's been there ever since she stepped off the train, a second-guessing that was just waiting for a reason to show itself. Her fear pours out: fear of uncertainty, fear of consequences, and fear of Henry and Quinn.

Scottie smiles, standing at the lectern, proud and happy to be stating her intentions—her aim for a legacy—and Dale realises she's no different to Scottie. This moment clarifies for Dale her own goals and reasons for being here. She, too, is in this for herself, as is possibly everyone here. This cause of Scottie's was only ever a place into which Dale could put her anger in the face of government control over her ovaries—control over her choice to have a family.

At some point in all of this, she's taken on Scottie's cause as her own, and she needs to let that go. This may be Scottie's legacy, but for Dale, this is about her own future. For Scottie, this is about the importance of cyborg technology over robot technology. For Dale, this is about stopping people like Quinn controlling people like herself.

Scottie continues, 'But first, we need to gain attention. We need to blow shit up.'

A sudden and unexpected roar of clapping and cheering erupts. The members stand and stomp and whistle in a release of tension.

Scottie waves them back into their seats. 'Dale has information on two companies that intend to employ robots as staff en masse, and when I say employ, I don't mean paid employment. These businesses enforce inequality and mistreat robots not only through slavery but through sex slavery.'

Heads turn to Dale with faces lit up and grinning. She's never experienced this sense of camaraderie in her life before, ever. She's never belonged to a community whose members hold the same ideas in their minds at once, and in doing so, lift each other's spirits. Dale feels that lift now. She smiles—a fervent grin to show that her confidence is equal to Scottie's. If ever there were signs that what they are doing here is bigger than ego, and bigger than Scottie's desire for a legacy or her own desire to have a family, this is it: these faces—who, like her, are frightened for their own reasons— are here, together as one. She sits up tall in her seat and lifts her face to them.

'We're up against big business,' Scottie continues. 'So, it requires a major disruption to get their attention. This makes some of you uncomfortable, I know, but we need to disrupt, starting with picketing; we'll sabotage them by entering buildings and going where we aren't invited; and we'll cause damage. You have to understand...' Scottie leans in and whispers, 'These are the most effective avenues available to us.'

Dale smiles at the nodding heads, and suddenly, she understands the irony of the moment. The idea of disruption for change could have come straight out of Henry's mouth. He spoke about the stepping stones, the mathematics between who we are and what we might become, but he neglected the human interference in it all—the link between who we are and what, through intimacy with our own creations, we might become. If Henry had any balls, he'd put his efforts where his mouth is and take a stand over the decimation of memory, history and heritage that he claims to value so much. He'd engender disruption and alter trajectories. But he doesn't. He sits back and ponders, vaguely, how much he loves his car.

'It needs to be understood,' Scottie says, 'that this isn't about defending these robots. This is about defending the relationships we have with each other as members of the human race. As lines blur between robot and human, the fiction and reality in our lives blur too, and so will our relationships. How will you be treated? How do you want to be treated? With respect, or with indifference or worse, contempt?'

Dale stands. She feels a need to contribute, to test her commitment, to be rallied by the presence of her own tribe and to walk out the door tonight feeling a part of this, not a fearful shadow. She grabs Scottie's attention with a pointed finger.

'Dale?' Scottie queries.

'We need to begin to communicate now,' Dale explains. 'Once Scottie begins to state our ideals to the public, you're to bring these up on your social media, in your friendship groups, and if you can, with your business contacts. Use Scottie's Twitter posts as your reference point. We want to get ahead of this and inform the public of our views, so that when they see the media images of our disruption and damage, they'll already be in a position to understand who we are and what we're about. When we take action, it's important to immediately and publicly claim each act. Scottie will do this officially by releasing streams to the media, but you can talk about this as soon as you get confirmation. Many will be moved to support us, and many will be moved to join us. And those who denigrate us? We do not engage, nor show them fear.' Dale hears her own voice falter at the word *fear*; she pauses, and then chooses not to own it. 'Those who denigrate us serve no purpose,' she concludes. 'We leave them behind in the dust of our actions.'

'What do you mean by "damage"?' asks a voice from the back seats.

'We'll get to the details soon,' Scottie answers.

'I mean, are you talking violence? Is that what you're saying?'

'We'll do whatever it takes.'

This is the kind of talk Scottie and Dale had feared, but it needs to be aired and discussed before they move ahead. While it was only her and Scottie, Dale revelled in the bliss of developing their plans, refining them over late nights together and expanding ideas on how they'd create a public furore. It energised her. Dale has been reluctant to grow their campaign beyond theory, but she thinks Scottie is right to expand the group now and create a following. It's time to set their baby free.

Scottie seems to have endless energy for the campaign. Not once has she wavered, shown signs of weakness or fatigue, or been in need of time to reflect. Even today, she keeps up the momentum of her speech: 'We're talking about stopping a machine that people see as a fascinating and fun idea,' she says. 'One that's backed financially and enmeshed in business and government. These robotics businesses are supported by high-profile leaders with money on their minds. They don't care about human welfare or culture or the health of the community. They tell us robots will be good for us all. They lie. There's only one way to stop this. We must make an impact. We'll do something that grabs attention, and we'll hurt those who invest in it—financially and emotionally. I'm afraid this means we need to cause damage; we need to be destructive. We need to force the pendulum to swing so far off-centre that it crashes like a demolition ball on its way back through.'

Scottie stares into the silence as uncertainty rumbles through the room. The members shift in their seats that creak and scrape on the floor.

'People will get hurt,' Scottie responds quietly in answer to the change in the room.

They listen.

Scottie sits down on the step before them all. 'We will incite anger, and I guarantee you, they will fight us. We'll be organised, and I promise you we'll also be backed by research and finance. We're starting small, in our own town. We'll disable the two newest businesses that intend to employ robots: QRC's Project City and Benny Liberanski's Uncanny Valley Club. We can't stop these people, they'll pick up and go on, but we *will* gain attention and followers—and this is our aim. We'll become monstrous in our own way. We must be united, and there can be no cracks.'

Dale feels the change of this moment. She's enjoyed the secretive nature of Scottie's plans and finding a purpose she could put her all into. It's been an outlet for her frustration with her losing the choice to be a mother. She's loved working with Scottie, and it occurs to Dale, as she sits in this room in the basement of the

Fuennel Industries building, that their actions may come to be more significant than she envisaged.

They're about to crush this fascination the community has with robot creation. It's an idea that has a strange hold over people's attention, and they're about to call into question the morality of this amusement with AI. It feels like they're exposing an evil embedded in a fairy tale—one that nobody has wanted to wake up to and recognise.

24

Dale & Scottie

They like Scottie's ideas, and a vibration of excitement moves through the room. They glance at each other and clap. The uncertain members remain mute and wide-eyed. Dale is encouraged that, for the most part, they're all still planted in their sweaty seats.

'And I plan to run for local government,' Scottie announces.

Scottie comes to a stop to let them take in this new information. For the interns, the move from theory to action is a vast leap, with no foreseeable net to catch them if things turn bad. It's not a leap they imagined taking while they watched reruns of *Blade Runner* and wrote their theses on cyborgs. Dale doubts serious politics were ever on their minds.

Scottie laughs at the stillness that takes over the room. 'Don't stress.' She fans the room with her hands. 'I don't expect I'll win any elections. There'll be lots of attention and no responsibility. The point is that we'll gain a lot of media attention by being loud and controversial, but also political. For us, a political party is about our visibility. We need to be seen. So, let's move past this and create a name for our party.'

'Let's keep it simple,' Thalia says. She's been quieter lately; it's unusual to hear her speak up.

The room turns to look at her. Dale is heartened by Thalia's interest in naming the political party. Of all the things she could put her name to, this one will be set in stone. Perhaps it's a sign of where Thalia sees her place in the movement—original creator.

'Instead of using the clunky "Enhance Not Replace" Twitter title for the party name,' Thalia suggests, 'what about The Cyborg Party?'

Thalia's retreat from her active involvement over the previous months has been a disappointment for Dale. She catches Thalia's eye, and the sense of camaraderie that's been absent comes flooding back. In the beginning, Thalia had been approachable when Scottie wasn't. Dale considers Thalia to be a mentor. She's missed the feeling of having an ally.

'Perfect,' Scottie declares. 'The Cyborg Party.' She smiles at Thalia.

Those two, Scottie and Thalia, began this movement together, so in some ways, they alone can take credit for what has been achieved. But now that Thalia has chosen a more voice-of-reason role, hovering on the outskirts of action, Dale has felt a need to step into that void left by Thalia. It feels right for her to do so. Everyone eventually finds their place in this according to their skill set, like water coming to settle.

≈

The last of them trail out of the room, shuffling and scooting each other as though they can't get out quick enough. They take the nervous tension with them out the door.

Scottie left first to avoid further discussion. She spoke her final words, stepped off the podium and was out the door before anyone had time to approach her. When the interns get a chance, they surround Scottie as if she's a cult leader. They want, or need, to be close to her, but Scottie promotes transparency in these planning meetings. If it needs to be said, it's to be said openly, for everyone to hear. She has no time for one-on-one conversations that may waste her time.

In the quiet of the room, on her own, Dale waits. A coolness rises around her now that everyone has left. It's late evening, and the cold seeps through the uninsulated walls and rises from the rickety floor. She can see this room collapsing one day, with them all in it, immortalised in the dust—the feminists of the 21st century.

It's only minutes before Scottie glides back in. She grins, floating on the success of the meeting, and she pulls Dale from her seat and wraps her long arms around her in a firm embrace. Dale breathes out loudly with an emotion-filled rush of air. Her eyes prickle with unexpected tears.

Scottie pushes her to arm's length and looks at her. 'Are you okay? I know, I know; this is a lot to take in.'

'I don't know where that came from.' Dale laughs and shakes off Scottie's firm hands. One bit of affection from Scottie and her courage sighed out of her. 'It's nothing; the energy in the room, I guess—the reality that it's finally happening.'

She's never thought of Scottie as the nurturing kind, but she *is* their leader, in a suffragette kind of way. When this word 'suffragette' finds its way into her thoughts, she has a sudden need to explain to Scottie what happened with Henry, because although it's been her private island of worry, it's connected to what they're in the midst of now with their newly formed party.

'I'm glad you're here,' Scottie says. 'With Thalia taking a break, you've become integral to us moving forward. It wouldn't be going so well without you.' Scottie steps back and takes a seat, still inspiringly tall even while sitting. 'Look what I've brought us.' Scottie lifts the lid off the last desk, pulls out a bottle of champagne and waggles it at Dale with her eyebrows raised. 'Time to celebrate, Dale. This is it, the beginning of a better future.'

Dale laughs. 'Just a small one for me.'

Scottie pours two glasses full to the brim. 'No skimping on celebrations,' she says. 'Now tell me what's on your mind. You've been sitting on something these last few days. I can hear it in your voice. Tell me and get it out of your system. I'll need you to be clear-headed from here on in.'

'You're right. I'm working through an idea, and I'd like your opinion on it.'

Scottie's smile relaxes. 'What've you got to tell me?' She passes Dale a very full glass of champagne, with bubbles zinging out of the top.

'What I'm about to tell you, Scottie, might be of use to us in this campaign,' she says, and leans in to her drink to sip it before she spills it.

Scottie lifts herself up to sit on the desk. Dale's skin prickles at having Scottie's full attention. She'd believe it if Scottie told her she could see right through her skin and into her thoughts. Dale turns her back on Scottie and folds an auditorium seat down. She sits in it and smooths her skirt flat on her thighs. She's conscious of the style of clothing she's been wearing as a way to get into her identity. It has her feeling vulnerable, and she longs for her jeans and sneakers.

'I want to talk about our theories on relationships with robots,' Dale says.

'Okay. Will we need another bottle?'

'I know it's not the best time to get into this, but trust me, I need to get this nutted out with somebody soon, and you're the best somebody for the job. And yes, you'll definitely need another drink or two after I tell you this.'

Scottie pulls another bottle out of the desk and plonks it next to the first.

'How many bottles have you got in there?' Dale laughs.

Scottie lifts the lid to show three more bottles. 'Ready for any celebration,' she says. 'I thought Thalia might join us too, but I'm not sure she's ready to see this as a celebration.'

'Yeah, she's pulling away, isn't she? I get it; sometimes we need to stick to our lanes to get the job done.'

'You're right, Dale; I was concerned, but we don't need to agree about everything all the time. In fact, the best results come when ideas butt against each other. I'm grateful for Thalia's input.'

'Okay.' Dale takes in a deep breath. She'd like to get this conversation over and done with. 'So, we humans have a tendency to anthropomorphise robots. Actually, we anthropomorphise everything from vacuums to cars; I've even named my vacuum—Elliot, in case you were wondering. And our behaviour and connections with said robot may reflect or be replicated in our human relationships, right?

'Yep,' Scottie concurs, 'I'm with you.'

'We form habits and patterns in relating, so it makes sense that behaviours a person develops in a relationship with their robot can transfer, or mimic, behaviours in their relationships with humans. This is our base theory, right? Fiction and reality blur, so what's working well with the robot might influence our human relationships.'

Scottie drains her whole glass before she answers. Her face has become white, drained of her usual colour. Flecks of sweat pool on her upper lip. 'Are you in a relationship with a robot, Dale?'

'Of course not.' Dale is insulted, but it's too funny, so she laughs.

'Okay, I shouldn't have even thought it, but you never know. So, we're talking hypothetically?'

'Yes, hypothetically. I'm thinking along the lines that if the person's behaviour with the robot is rewarded, they then—'

'It's complex, isn't it?' Scottie interjects. 'So many new threads of relating can come out of relationships with robots. This is the whole point of our cause, isn't it? We need to slow this down and encourage people to think it through before we plough headlong into a new way of living with robots. We need regulation around these kinds of relationships, but that's a whole other campaign.'

'Okay.' Dale's urge to blurt it all out overwhelms her. 'Scottie, I'll explain it to you exactly, and I'm sorry, but I lied: it's not hypothetical. This is real. I've seen it. I've felt it. I'm living it. I'm seeing a real and up-close application of our theory in action. It's Henry; he has a problem.'

'Everyone knows about Henry's problem, Dale. I don't see what you're getting at.' Scottie blinks once, twice, in what appears to be agitation. She's probably tired now, and wanting to go home, not get involved in a complex discussion.

Dale, on the verge of changing her mind, looks at the door.

'I can see your mind turning this over. Just blurt it out and let me decide if it's something we should be in turmoil about.' Scottie laughs.

Dale takes a long drink. 'I think Henry bought a sex doll. I mean, I know that he did. I saw the box, and I saw her in his home when I broke in.'

'Okay, that's no surprise, though, is it? He's about to manage the biggest robot city in the state's history. I'd be more surprised if he *didn't* own one, or twenty for that matter, in every colour.' Scottie snorts.

'I think he purchased it to help with his ED.'

'So, we're talking about the positives of sex-doll ownership? This is not helpful to us right now. I know there are positives, but we're focussed on the bigger picture, the humanity—'

'No, hear me out, Scottie. Let me go back to the start. Henry and I began a relationship, together...with... each other.'

'I thought as much. I mean, I knew; you know how people talk. Listen, Dale, I'm not comfortable with it, but it is what it is—as long as you're clear about your job here with us, and you understand that nobody asked you nor expected you to do that. You know that, right?'

Dale's confidence scatters at the thought that Scottie may feel let down by her connection with Henry. She shakes it off and finds her harder self. 'So, being close to Henry, I know that he'd been suffering from a serious problem, and then, after he'd taken in the sex doll, his issues switched to recovery. A wow of a recovery—sort of recovery amplified, if that's a thing.'

'Okay, I'm still not seeing the problem, Dale. Henry fixed himself; good for Henry. Not our business.' Scottie rests her chin in her hand, her elbow on her knee, waiting.

'Henry has recovered, but it's not in a healthy way. He's...more aggressive about it all.'

'Aggressive about what all? About your relationship?'

'Henry, well … we were out on a job, and he… he's difficult, you know? He's kind of closed off. I wanted more: a more collaborative relationship, a real relationship, sharing. We spoke about his problem. I think I pushed him further than he wanted—and he kind of wanted to prove himself, on me.'

'Okay, I'm … not following what it is you want to say to me.'

'He became frustrated, maybe angry? I don't know. Embarrassed? I was frustrated with him too. Like I said, he wanted to prove himself. Well, he did. He proved himself. He showed me.'

'Showed you? Showed you, what? He raped you? Is that what you're saying?'

Dale is silent. She holds Scottie's gaze.

When Scottie says the words 'He raped you', Dale slumps in her seat. She opens her mouth, but the words have gone. She touches her forehead and realises her fingers have become numb, as though the blood has rushed from her hands. She played this conversation out in her mind many times, and it was upsetting, but this bodily reaction frightens her. She becomes dizzy; she can't think.

Scottie stands up fast, and the chair collapses behind her.

Dale lets her feelings be what they are and sticks to her plan. 'And his problem appears to have gone away. I'm not looking for sympathy over this, Scottie; sit down. Let's talk about it. I want you to see the connection. His relationship with the sex doll was obviously one of superiority, maybe control? Power? Perhaps even violence? And now, he seems to believe this is the way he needs to be. You see? He seems to have discovered that overpowering, being powerful, ignites something in him.'

'Oh Dale.' Scottie rights her chair and sits again. 'I understand what you're saying.' She looks at Dale intently. 'Do you think Henry is so stupid as to not see what's happened?' She reaches for the bottle, fills her glass and upends it into her mouth.

Not knowing what else to say, Dale empties the bottle into her own glass. The celebratory tinkle into the glass makes her feel sick to her stomach. She lifts the glass to her lips. A gulp strains in her throat. Speaking it out loud has made it real—sickening.

'I don't think it's a matter of stupidity, or intelligence, Scottie. I think it happened, and it makes sense to him. I think he believes it's out of his hands. I never imagined he had it in him to be so—'

'He's betwixt and between.'

Dale looks at her feet, not understanding Scottie's comment.

'He's at the in-between space, neither in one space nor another: neither in the human nor the robot space. He's not acting under the laws of humans nor under the laws of robots—if there were such a thing—he's somewhere in the middle; he's betwixt and between.'

'You're right,' Dale says. 'He's fallen between the cracks. But you know what? He's not stupid, and at the end of the day, he knows what's right and what's wrong. He's human, and so am I.'

'I didn't mean for you to be in this kind of situation, Dale. To be honest, I'm having trouble imagining Henry…' She pauses. 'Henry is… um, Henry isn't really… he's not that kind of…' Scottie rubs her eyes. 'Are you okay, Dale? Have you been to the police?'

'No, I wanted to talk this through with you first.' Dale breathes in and takes a moment to order her words. What she says next will change everything. This is where she decides how deep in this she'll go. 'I was thinking, Scottie, we could use this. I could put this story on the website. I mean, we could use this to leverage our campaign. My story will make our point clearer to many people. It's evidence of everything we've been saying.'

Scottie puts her palms to her flushed cheeks. 'And here I was thinking your commitment had wavered, Dale. I thought having you spend time enmeshed in QRC meant I might lose you to them. Now you're telling me the opposite. I'm so very sorry. This is not a consequence we can accept. This is just… Have you thought this through? We need to think about the consequences of you putting your experience to the public. You need to put yourself first.'

'I'd rather use it for this than go down the uncertain path of charging him. It'll have more meaning this way.'

'We can do both: charge him and use it to support our movement.'

'No, Scottie. I don't want to give them a heads up. It needs to have its moment in public first.'

Scottie links her arm in Dale's. They stare at the white screen that still outlines their data. This moment, this here, is the solidarity that keeps Dale committed to their work—this belief in The Core—together.

'Okay,' Scottie concedes. 'Put something together for the blog when you're ready, and if you still want to go ahead with it, you can put it online yourself—not someone else. I want you to be in control of this and to be free to change your mind at any time.'

'I can do this, Scottie. This is important to me. I think we can use this to have them take a huge hit. It may be the thing we've been waiting for, as you say, to blow this shit right up.'

Scottie laughs, but her smile disintegrates quickly. 'Don't do this immediately. I want you to think hard about it, Dale—and I will too—and talk it though with Thalia. Have you told Thalia?'

'No, and I won't. There's such a thing as being too cautious. Thalia's heavy on the cons. She won't support me in this.'

'Dale.' Scottie stands, paces around the chairs, opens the second bottle and angles it into her glass. She nods at Dale. 'Listen, if you want to do this, great, but after this is over, you still have the option to have him charged.'

'Okay,' Dale says. 'Good. I'll write something, and then we'll talk about it again. But for now, let's put it aside. Have you got time to talk about the information I've managed to gather?'

'Sure, let's talk about that, but I mean it when I say you should sit on it for a while and not act. Let's look at what you're working on. What do you know about the Project City plans?'

'I accessed files from Henry's laptop in his apartment. I can't get near anything at QRC. I don't think they trust anyone, let alone a nobody intern like me.'

'Did you find any start dates or locations?'

Dale leans back in her seat. The champagne glows in her chest. 'I went with Henry to the site where they plan to build Project City.

He didn't say that's what it was, but I have no doubt that's where it is. The site's been cleared, and the paperwork shows the building works are to start next month. Henry has only recently been given the project manager position, and to tell you the truth, I'm not sure he's up to it.'

'Is The Uncanny Valley Club listed as a tenant of Project City?'

'It is.'

Scottie chuckles. 'What a mess that place will be. Have you seen any indication of where the QRC warehouse is situated?'

'I don't think Henry even knows where it is.'

'Listen, Dale, write your blog post, but don't post it. If you can hold off for a few days, I'll have the perfect video clip to go with it. Henry's not going to like you detailing his behaviour to the public, but he's definitely not going to enjoy the video of him I've procured. I think it's best you don't go back to work at QRC.'

'I'll make myself scarce. I feel like I've let everyone down, Scottie. Making Quinn's warehouse public was one of our goals, and I'm no closer to finding its location.'

Scottie raises her glass to Dale. 'It'd be great if we found it, but we have enough to work with now.'

Dale raises her champagne to Scottie in return. She feels energised. They clink glasses with gusto and step back as the glasses shatter and glinting shards fall to the floor between them. It feels exactly how it should: like the sealing of a pact between them.

25

Henry, Quinn & Benny

Henry searches Benny's face for a clue as to why this meeting in Quinn's office has been called. Benny slides down in his seat, his legs spread in opposite directions. He presses one hand firmly into his pocket, fiddling with something, while the other hand taps the air as though it's a piano.

'Hey Benn,' Henry says, 'would you know why Quinn's called us in here together?'

Benny shrugs. 'For an announcement? Something amazing?' He blows out air in boredom, flubbering it through his lips. 'Quinn never calls me in for meetings with you, Henry. We usually talk *about you*, not to you.' Benny laughs and pulls a lever to let his swivel chair drop to its base. 'Yep,' he says to nobody.

Benny gives off the vibe that he believes there's a hierarchy at QRC. One that looks like Benny is above Henry: first Quinn, then Benny, followed by Henry, next is perhaps Esther or Griff, and finally, everyone else. Throughout their regular sessions, Henry lets that version of QRC slide, but he's certain Benny has it wrong. In his mind it goes Quinn, Henry, a few other people, then Benny.

Henry presses his fingers into the grainy muscles in his neck and eyes Benny thoughtfully.

≈

This morning has become difficult. Henry's phone had rung from an unknown number that persisted. Then it rang from a different number that he didn't recognise. No sooner had it stopped when another number called, then another and another.

He listened to the first of the messages, pressing his ear against the phone until it hurt, to confirm what he heard, and then he dropped his phone to the floor. It cracked when it hit the tile. He flicked up the table-top screen and typed into the browser the name that had been repeated in the messages over and over: Enhance Not Replace.

As a result, Henry told Viv he needed to make a few changes. She looked at him with an easy swivel of her neck, and asked if she might assist with the changes he was about to make.

'You want to help me disable your own intelligence? You don't need to help,' he said gently, as though this was a kind concession. He wanted to be kind to her.

'What changes will you make?' she asked.

'Changes to your character and behavioural changes too. And I'm sorry, but you can't sleep with me in my bed anymore.'

'For how long?'

'Forever, maybe. Plus, I won't be calling you by your name any longer, as it's too personal, I'll call you by your model name, Domin, and I'll switch your empathy off.' He stopped himself from asking her if that would be okay. He pulled out his phone and tapped her app. He pressed C.

Select empathy settings.

Select intelligence settings.

Select.

Select.

Select.

He moved through the questions and reduced her personality to that of a dishwasher.

'You've removed the settings that make me compatible with you.' Domin smiled and turned to gaze absentmindedly out the window.

'I have to crawl back some ground here, Domin. I mean, what I do to you here in the privacy of our home is fine, but I've become…' He scrambled for an explanation of how time spent with her affected him. Her presence left him empty. Her predictability was exasperating and her obedience frustrating, but that wasn't her fault. She couldn't remedy that, and now, it no longer mattered. She's gone. Depriving Domin of intelligent conversation was wretched, but even more wretched was that he'd deprived *himself* of her conversation.

The words Dale used in her blog post to describe their relationship outlined an event that was foreign to him. It's true, they had been together, but they'd each lived through a completely different experience. He's sure he explained it to her. That it was a matter of … That he was sorry it had to be that way, and that he had to show her, because she pushed him. She said he was scared. She understood what happened. She didn't say anything else about it at the time.

His phone rang repeatedly.

'Your telephone has rung many times, Henry,' Domin observed, reporting to him like a machine would.

He turned to her and felt complete release when he did what he'd been wanting to do: he punched her. Hard. She dropped to the floor. He dragged her behind him to the kitchen, her legs and arms smacking furniture and bumping on the tiles. He searched in the kitchen drawers for a knife or scissors—for anything capable of inflicting good damage.

≈

'What do *you* think this is about?' Benny asks.

'Whatever it is, we shouldn't jump to conclusions about who's to blame,' Henry says.

'Blame? What's happened? What have you done, Henry? I'm sure *I* haven't done anything. In fact, all I've got for Quinn is good news.'

The lift door clangs as it opens, and Quinn's feet slap hard on the floor as he moves through the office. Whether they're angry steps or consolatory steps, Henry can't tell. Maybe purposeful steps —purposeful would be easier than angry.

Quinn spins on his feet and steps into the office. He takes a seat at his desk and turns to face Benny, and now Henry sees that, in fact, he, Henry, may be holding the lower position in the hierarchy. Benny swivels on his seat and faces Quinn, leaving Henry completely outside the triangle.

'Okay.' Quinn throws a hand over his desk and his screen lights up.

Henry has a rush of memories from the last few weeks: in the car with Dale out on the highway, that energy surge after whatever it was Scottie put in his coffee, the visit to The Uncanny Valley Club and his escalating violence with his Domin. They coincided with him conquering his problem, followed by a frenzied, spiralling, out-of-control series of encounters, like a sex addict on ice.

Henry toys with the idea that one different choice might have changed everything, and that he wouldn't now be the third wheel in the office. Ultimately, it's Benny's fault. If Benny hadn't encouraged him to spend those few hours there with Kimset—all that blood on the floor—then he wouldn't have taken Dale off the side of the road to show her how things were to be done now.

'So, this has happened.' Quinn drags his hand slowly over his head with a hand full of comb-over, then spins the screen around with a flippant slap of the back of his hand for them to see.

And there it is: Scottie's website and Dale's blog post. So eloquent, so descriptive and so damaging. Quinn turns it to Henry.

'I've seen it,' Henry confesses, and then puts his hand to his forehead. That's all he can do. Apologising will never be enough.

'What is it?' Benny says, and he jumps to his feet. Benny's face has turned white, probably due to being nettled that Henry knows something he doesn't.

Quinn swivels the screen to Benny with an annoyed flick of his hand. 'Scottie Fuennel's website.'

'So? We've all seen that; there's nothing but self-indulgent cyborgy and propaganda there.'

'Have you read it today, Benny? Tell him, Henry. Tell him what you did.' Quinn doesn't look at Henry while he speaks. His face contorts with an unreadable emotion.

'He can read it for himself,' Henry responds.

'Well, somebody tell me,' Benny demands, and then sits back in his seat.

'This,' Quinn says, 'is damaging media for us. Can you believe this blog post written by Dale? Who, by the way, appears to have disappeared from the face of the earth—no surprise there. The post outlines—in very specific detail, I might add—a little rendezvous she had with Henry, which she is calling a rape.'

Quinn waves his hand at Henry, a kiss of air reaches him, cooling his sweaty face. Quinn stands. Henry watches his feet walk to the window. The edges of his grey suit pants sweep the floor with their stringy, bedraggled hems.

'The blog goes on to talk about her relationship with Henry, and it gives a description of Henry's liaisons with a social bot and the supposed effect it had on him. She draws a connection to the violence toward her at Henry's hands.' Quinn taps the window with a finger, in thought. 'They're making little connections here, and here, and here'—Quinn pokes the air randomly about him—'as though this is a thing.' He turns to look at Henry and Benny, his face aghast.

Benny nods at Henry, now including him in their triangle. The look on Benny's face is of wonder. He leans forward and slaps Henry on the knee. 'So, we fixed your Little Problem then, Henry?' He rocks backward and forward in his seat, like he's sitting on something good. 'Told you we would. Didn't I tell you, Quinn?'

Henry rubs his face with his palms. He sighs and swallows a lump of air. There's nothing he can say. His reputation has gone to shit. He'll lose his job. He won't work in this town again, or in this hemisphere. Nobody will take him on. He'll be forced to leave.

'For fuck's sake, Henry,' Quinn says. 'How could you let her write this stuff?'

Henry points a finger to himself. 'Me?' he squeaks.

'Of course,' Quinn states. 'You... you need to get control of this. I don't believe a word of it. It's all bullshit. The lying cow. But it's the damage I'm concerned about—damage to the business. People will believe this shit. We need to respond, and we need to act with an equal and appropriate reply. Henry, there's no easy way out of this. You'll need to apologise with a great big, heartfelt, humble, wet apology. Can you cry on demand? Can you do that, Henry?'

Benny giggles, slips further down in his seat and grins at Henry, his silky, black hair flipping and shimmying about like a velveteen curtain.

'I'm prepared to do what it takes to make it right,' Henry replies, knowing there's not much he can do to fix it.

'Let's get Esther in; we need her to clean this up.' From behind his desk, Quinn calls out, 'Esther! Esther!' There's no answer, and he steps out the doorway and screams her name, '*Essstthhherr!*

Her voice screams back, unintelligible, but in a tone somewhere between annoyance and indifference. 'We've got a problem, Esther; get Olly in, will you?'

Benny laughs louder, folding his arms and sitting back in his chair, probably enjoying Henry's discomfort.

'Not really a laughing matter, eh, Benny?' queries Quinn. 'You might think this is funny, but this is possibly the end of your business too, you know. I can find other outlets to take on Project City's dolls, and thankfully, the warehouse hasn't been named, but Dale wrote about your business. Your club will suffer because of this.'

Quinn leans forward and points at the screen. 'Right here, Benny. Your name. It's right here: Benny Liberanski, social robot salesman. And Project City and The Uncanny Valley Club—all named. And this… this is the worst. I can't even watch this. Benny, how did this video happen? This is in your club, yes?' Quinn paces backward and forward in the small office space. He trips over one of Benny's feet and recovers by slapping a hand on his desk. 'I can't even watch the whole thing, but I bet I'm the only person who hasn't watched it, except for you pair of knobs. At least you're slow, Henry, and Project City hasn't got off the ground yet. But the name… We'll need to change the name. Benny, stop laughing, have you no idea what's happening here?'

Benny stands up and places his hands on his hips. 'I know exactly what's happened here, Quinn. Are you thinking of letting poor Henry go? Is that what's happening here?' Benny comes to stand behind Henry and grabs him by both shoulders. 'This poor guy, this guy we set up like a guinea pig—you can't just dump him like that. We need to stick by him.' He shakes Henry's shoulders, and his fingernails dig into flesh.

'This guy, Quinn—our Henry—do you know what he's done for us all? You're the one who has no idea, Quinn. Even I had no idea; no idea at all. This morning, my sales numbers moved dramatically, and I mean moved like a shot, and I was thinking, *What have I done to get my sales moving? Whatever's happened, I need to repeat it.* I had no idea it was all Henry's doing; that his humiliation, his little bad-boy behaviour, his Little Problem, had found its way to daylight. I mean, look at this; will you just fucking look at this?' Benny pulls his phone from his pocket and pokes at it. 'Fucking look at this graph, Quinn. My sales from the last day—they're fucking through the roof. I can't keep up with the orders. I mean, Henry and his humiliation have sent my sales skyrocketing. Bring on the bad press! People love this shit. Shake the man's hand, Quinn!' Benny grabs Henry's hand and shakes it, pumping it up and down, up and down. 'Bring it on, bad-boy Henry!'

'Stop it, Benny.' Quinn swivels his seat to face Henry. He smiles at him as if Henry's moved to the top position in their little hierarchy.

≈

Henry thinks of Viv, who's back in his apartment. He thinks of her twisted body and her bent arms. He thinks of the legs that he yanked until the wires broke free, and of her vacant, black holes for eyes that he gauged with a kitchen knife. He thinks of the way he laid her arms, legs, torso and head on top of each other until she was a pile of plastic and wire, oozing strawberry blood from her knees, from her eyes, from her elbows, her sweet scent filling the cupboard.

26

Dale

Dale sits in the window seat at Café Bang-Bang. Anyone who'd sat here before her and looked out this window would be oblivious to the manufacturing that goes on just across the road, beyond the purple and yellow creepers that cover the stark concrete wall.

It occurs to Dale that it's possible the chemical waste from the QRC warehouse has quietly been disappearing into the flowing river that sits beyond the building. Her phone vibrates in her lap. She glances at it. A message from Scottie at this point isn't a part of their tightly choreographed plan. Her instinct is not to look, and when she does look, she wishes she hadn't. She wishes she didn't know the information in the message.

She curls her hair behind her ears and is surprised to feel her hands are shaking. She rests her arms on the table, either side of her coffee, and alternates between watching the warehouse through the window and glancing at her phone. The quiet background murmur in the café—plates being stacked and coffee gurgling—comforts her. She makes a note of the time to the second: 1:56 and 36 seconds, 37, 38, 39 …

And she waits.

Last night, at Scottie's request, she typed a concise message for the Enhance Not Replace blog. Two sentences, which once the allotted time arrives, will be released to the public—a sweet shout-out to the world that they, The Cyborg Party, are laying claim to recent activist events. From then, their conversation with the community begins, about a just and sound future in robotics.

Once she had finished writing the blog post, she shut down the browser, pinched down the screen and went about her night in her usual way. She ate a meal of simple poached eggs and rocket; brushed her teeth; watched her pupils in the mirror—bulging, retreating, bulging and retreating in a reflection of her alternating anxiety and her sense of achievement; and went to bed.

She sank her head into her pillow and fell into a deep sleep, but she woke suddenly, hours later, to words colliding about in her thoughts as though they'd been doing the work while she slept. Words jumped and rearranged themselves until they fell in a manner that explained the upcoming protests in a better format than she had written earlier for the blog—words that could help people understand what it is Scottie stands for, and why they had done what they're about to do.

In hindsight, the few concise words she'd typed earlier were never going to be enough. She went back to her screen, and in the early hours of the morning, she brought to her fingers the sense of anger, frustration and concern for the future. She worked with passion until four in the morning. She explained the philosophy behind their act because, after all, the act without explanation might be mistaken for tit-for-tat revenge against Quinn and Henry for her rape. She explained their actions will create a point in history that will draw all eyes back to Scottie and the entire movement. She explained how it is they came to take this extreme position, and that their actions at this moment create the platform on which to launch into a more positive future. It became a very long post, but one she was more satisfied with.

≈

The glass in every window in Café Bang-Bang shudders, then there's a crack so loud that her ears ring. Staff behind Dale in the café drop suddenly to the floor and seek cover under tables and counters. Even though Dale has anticipated this, she drops her cup to the table in complete shock. Coffee spills, and shivering drips run into her lap.

Out in the street, sprouting from the bombed warehouse roof like a volcanic eruption, is a brilliant visual of projecting torsos, ranging in colours from orange to pink to brown to green to black. Out shoot legs, arms and heads in varying stages of smouldering degradation, and melted plastics warped out of shape splatter against the footpath. Hands and fingers plop at random in the middle of the road among the traffic that pulls to an astounded stop. Arms drooping and bending at odd angles fly through the air. Singed hair floats on the breeze, this way and that, coming to settle upon cars, manicured lawns and people, who pluck at it cautiously with pincer fingers. Sturdy skeletons glint in the sunlit afternoon as they are flung into the air, then plummet to the lawns, piercing the earth to stand erect like artistic political statements.

Dale strokes her screen. Touching her finger to the appropriate tabs, she releases the long blog post she wrote last night. She's overcome with relief, then joy, and finally, a sense of accomplishment. She snaps a picture through the window with her phone. This extraordinary image will be a perfect visual for the media.

She raises her cup to her lips and drains what's left of her coffee.

The breathy, frightened speech of the waitress rushes against the back of her neck. 'Oh my God! What's happened?'

The café staff and customers run forward in a pressing stampede to witness this confusing and monstrous explosion.

Dale imagines how it looks from their eyes, fresh and without the knowledge of planning it. It's likely these people had no idea that Quinn's warehouse sat right across the road from them while they sipped at their coffee and poked at their meals. Feeling the intensity of the ground-shaking bomb and witnessing body parts fleeing across the sky has sent them into confusion.

'They're not real bodies,' Dale says, to relieve them of their anxiety. 'You're safe. It's a robotics factory.'

The waitress's eyes dart about the street as though she expects a terrorist to declare themselves.

I'm here, right here. Your terrorist is here.

'Should we call the police?' the waitress asks of no one in particular.

'I'll do it,' Dale offers. She lifts her phone and hits speed dial, soon connecting with an operator at the emergency-services switchboard to explain the situation.

'Yes, an explosion,' she confirms. 'I don't really know.' Then, she adds, 'I've heard that an activist group have claimed the bombing. Somebody said The Cyborg Party.'

Dale follows the café staff as they spill out into the street and take comfort in discussing the explosion with businesses up and down the curb. They speak in awe about this warehouse across the road that they've discovered. Dale listens, taking their comments as compliments for a job well done. She has an urge to say, 'I did this; I did this magnificent thing.'

It's a striking picture, Dale thinks as she, too, gazes over the rainbow-coloured body parts. She goes back inside the café to sit down and take it all in, and to take a moment to feel the experience. Soon, there will be consequences.

She raises her phone and takes a panoramic video, getting in everything she can see from the left of the street to the right. Then, she watches it back to herself, feeling happy; it's all played out as they'd hoped.

She deletes the message Scottie had sent to her: 'Where are you, Dale? Halt the bombing. We need to stop it; there are complications! Some of Quinn's warehouse dolls have biological organs.'

27

Henry

The opening of The Uncanny Valley Club is big, loud and frenzied. Proud Llama, the digital DJ celebrity, emcees the event for Benny. 'Flamboyant' is the only description Henry can come up with when he imagines describing it to Viv.

Benny sidles up to Henry, nodding excitedly. 'Look, look, look what I did!' he says.

The music is erratic and disruptive, and Henry can't entertain anything near a proper conversation.

'Proud Llama is here, did you see?' Beads of sweat form on Benny's upper lip when he speaks about Proud Llama, and later, watching him talk to it, Henry can see that Benny is a submissive puddle of adoration in its presence.

Benny slaps Henry on the shoulder and moves off to speak to someone more interesting. Henry presses himself to the wall. It's crowded, and as significant as the venue is to him, he himself is insignificant to every other person present.

Proud Llama kicks things off with a baseball bat swung at a naked robot piñata, beating the thousands of goodies into the crowd.

A frenzy of dolls and people fight with shoulders and shoves, teeth and boots, for the spray that rains down on the crowd.

Henry doesn't understand the frenzy over the contents of the piñata until the feasting is over; the piñata is a sad, deflated pile of rubbish; and the entire place has become a drug-enhanced, writhing orgy. Henry longs for the quiet of his apartment and the company of his Viv.

≈

Henry turns the key and slides the padlock from the cupboard handle. He feels the smooth metal in his fingers. These movements are tactile and hold him poised in this moment. Whatever he's done is past, whatever happens now is fine and whatever comes will come.

He opens the cupboard door.

Viv's head sits on top of the pile of her body parts, her neck held at a chastising angle as if she's about to accuse him, as though she's waited patiently for this exact moment—the moment he changes his mind. But she doesn't move and hasn't done since he pushed her in there. Her thighs press against her cheeks, her feet curled stupidly backward over her head. There's not a single flicker of recognition from her eyes.

A shift in his world has given him permission to come back to her. But he still has mixed feelings about her—lust and hate—for what she is and what she isn't. He's horribly aware that she made him who he is now—*she* created *him*. He's connected to her in an unexpected and eternal way.

He takes her by one leg, shuffles backward and drags her out. She glides out across the floor as one pile of parts, connected by threads of veins, her limp head lolling and her tongue flapping. When he imagines it's possible to repair her, he feels the emotional weight of it all lift.

He dumps Viv by the screen and watches the images which have been played all morning, of damaged robot bodies strewn across an immaculate green lawn. He expects to be approached for a meeting soon to initiate plans to respond to this disaster, but he's in no hurry to deal with Benny, or Quinn. His phone will ring soon enough.

In the centre of this pile that is Vivify, her eyes are still, like stagnant water. Her head sits, sunken into her pile of parts, like a swami trying to climb into herself. She slumps in a pool of her own sweet blood. He picks up her hands, still silky, and places them spread outward, like a starfish. He tugs her legs straight, placing her ankles together in a Jesus pose. He turns her head upright and pulls it to straighten and lengthen her neck.

In his office, he slides open the cupboard door. He sifts through the items to look for the kit, finding the never used robo-vac, the unopened home web-hub, the Thief-No-More security system, the space drone he was supposed to test drive, and the 15 unwrapped birthday gifts from his father. He takes out the robo-kit that he coerced Benny into taking from Quinn's warehouse.

He begins at her feet.

Seated cross-legged on the floor, he takes her right ankle and rests it in his lap. It flops sideways. He smiles at the idea that he's a modern Geppetto, and Viv is his puppet. He understands the damage he's done to her body. If he's inclined to, he'll tell her he did it to give her freedom—freedom from the treatment she'd receive as a non-human. It'll be his excuse, even though that isn't really how it was. He was afraid of the power she held over him. That combination of fascination and fear was powerful.

He breathes in. The thing he's noticed the most since Scottie slipped him that drug-laden coffee is a clarity of mind and depth of thought that has him inclined to philosophise about the simplest of things.

He flinches at a knock at the door. A key scrapes in the lock, and the beat in his chest calms. Since Dale's blog post, the threats he's received in her defence have been constant and violent, and they come from unexpected places. He's always on edge now, and it's caused him to agonise over whether he'll lie to Quinn about what he ultimately did for Scottie and her Core, and stay at QRC, or find a new life away from here—away from all of them.

Vince is tall. He strides through the door, this brand of Vince that Henry is yet to tire of.

'What's this?' Vince asks, with his hands in his pockets and a nod at Viv.

Henry's phone vibrates. He looks at it. Scottie has sent him a video, and with it a short note: 'Come see me. I have something for you, by way of thanks.' The video is more of the same that he's already seen: of the shattered warehouse, with images of a Butler thrashing about on the manicured lawn, gathering up limbs, torsos and fingers, and then rushing in a flurry to drop them in a pile beyond the concrete walls of the roofless warehouse. Scottie sends a laughing emoji with it. She's been enjoying these videos for some time.

Henry deletes both this video and the text he sent to her with the warehouse address given to him by Benny. He hopes she's done the same. *New Beginnings* is the title Scottie gave this little video. He gives this idea thought. The destruction of the warehouse will be a mere hiccup for Quinn, but perhaps it's a beginning for some.

'Are you okay?' Vince queries.

'Of course.'

'I mean about Quinn.'

'Quinn?'

Vince flicks up his phone screen and holds it up for Henry to see. 'Yes, Quinn,' Vince repeats, in echo with a journalist on the screen, who is standing before the still-smouldering warehouse: 'The human body found in the rubble is that of the owner of the warehouse. The investigation is now a murder inquiry. We're waiting to learn who it is that will be held responsible for Quinn's death.'

Julie Proudfoot is an author of fiction, poetry and non-fiction. Her first published novel, The Neighbour, won the Seizure Viva La Novella Prize. Julie has appeared at Bendigo Writers Festival, Queenscliffe Literary Festival, Perth Writers Festival, and The Melbourne Emerging Writer's Festival. She draws on her degrees in Psychology, Anthropology and Philosophy to inform her work. Julie writes from her home in Queensland, Australia.

Bibliography

Richardson, K. (2015). *An Anthropology of Robots and A.I.* Routledge, New York, NY.

Levy, D. (2007). *Love and Sex with Robots: The evolution of human-robot relationships.* Harper Collins, New York, NY.

Turkle, S. (1984). *The Second Self: Computers and the human spirit.* Simon and Schuster, Inc., New York, NY.

Freud, S. (2003). *The Uncanny.* Penguin, London, UK.

Wood, G. (2003). *Living Dolls: A magical history of the quest for mechanical life.* Gardners Books, Eastbourne, UK.

Thank you

Thank you to the authors of books and other works that were part of my reading to inspire and inform The Uncanny Valley Club (as mentioned in the bibliography), but in particular, Dr Kathleen Richardson, and Sherry Turkle. Thank you to Daniel Young, editor of Tincture Journal, for his insightful thoughts as first reader. Thank you to the town of Agnes Water whose healing properties of warmth and sun and sea-spray and animals and plants and wind and rain enabled me to complete the book after much illness kept it on ice for some time. Thank you to editor, Lindsay Corten of Corten Editorial, who read and polished until it shone, whose diligent and dedicated work gave the book confidence and wings. Thank you to my children who support and ask about the work, and make me smile, and especially thank you to Wayne who always, always stands by me, and the work, and reads and reads until his eyes burn.